Without Hats, Who Can Tell the Good Guys?

Mildred Ames

Without Hats, Who Can Tell the Good Guys?

E. P. Dutton & Co., Inc.   □   New York

Library of Congress Cataloging in Publication Data

Ames, Mildred   Without hats, who can tell the good guys?

SUMMARY: Convinced he will never get used to
his new foster family, a young boy dreams of the day
his father will come to take him away.

[1. Foster home care—Fiction.   2. Family life—Fiction]
I. Title.
PZ7.A5143Wi   [Fic]   75-33635   ISBN 0-525-43125-x

Published simultaneously in Canada by Clarke,
Irwin & Company Limited, Toronto and Vancouver

Designed by Meri Shardin
Printed in the U.S.A.   First Edition
10 9 8 7 6 5 4 3 2 1

To Margaret, Annie, and Cliff

Contents

Without Hats, Who Can Tell the Good Guys?

1

Welcome Aboard

Anthony Lang, Jr. sat on the edge of the bed, feeling much younger than his eleven years. As he watched Mrs. Diamond unpack his things, the old empty-hungry feeling came over him. Yet it wasn't hunger, he knew. Instead, the hollow felt like an enormous lump that left no room for food.

"I just know you're going to like your bedroom, Anthony." Mrs. Diamond gave him a toothy smile. "We fixed it up real special. Did you see the desk? Mr. Diamond found that at the Goodwill store. He sanded it down and stained it and put two coats of boat varnish on it. Why, I just don't guess anyone could tell it from new now, do you?"

"Looks nice." Anthony tried to sound more interested than he was. He knew he was lucky to have a room of his own. At the Sauters' he'd had to share a room with Petey, their youngest son. Now, even the thought of the privacy he had so craved was not enough to drive away that big lump in his stomach.

Mrs. Diamond lifted a box from the old suitcase that had once belonged to Anthony's father. "Oh, my, isn't this pretty!"

"It was my mother's. It's a Chinese puzzle box." Anthony watched her anxiously as she stared down at the painting on top, a willow beside a stream with a picturesque bridge. Then she turned the box around to admire the rows of parquetry that covered the sides and alternated with strips of hand-painted designs.

"A puzzle box—I'll bet that's fun." She obviously thought it a toy. "I'll just put it in one of your drawers."

Anthony decided he would move the box to a different drawer later. Not that anyone could tell from looking at it that each of those rows along the sides slid open, one at a time. And only if you knew the right order. It called for about twenty different operations and had taken forever for him to learn. Now the box held all the money he had in the world, over twenty dollars. With that kind of money, you could feel a little independent. Twenty dollars would buy a lot of hamburgers (or was it peanuts that held more nourishment for the money?) if you ever wanted to run away.

"What's this?" Mrs. Diamond asked, holding a cardboard box now.

"A P–51 model. Mr. Sauter gave it to me before I left."

"Well! Now wasn't that nice of him!" She sounded as

if she was trying hard to act excited about everything.

"When I put it together, it'll look just like the picture on the cover."

With a fleeting glance at the sleek, silver plane on top, she gushed, "You don't say!" then absently placed the box on the Goodwill desk. "Well, now, I guess that about does it." She started to close the suitcase.

Anthony sprang to his feet, feeling a little panicky. "The picture—it's there, isn't it?"

"Picture?" Mrs. Diamond opened the suitcase again. "I don't see—well, what do you know? Almost missed it all turned upside down that way." To Anthony's great relief, she drew out his most precious possession and turned it over to find two happy faces smiling up at her. "Well! I just bet I know who this is—your mom and dad." When Anthony nodded, she said, "We'll just sit this right here on top of the dresser where you can see them real good." She stood back and stared at them again. "Well, aren't they nice looking."

The picture was an old one, taken soon after his mother and father had married. Somehow the sight of their familiar, smiling faces in that strange house, that strange room, made the lump inside him grow bigger instead of smaller.

"They look so young and happy." Mrs. Diamond gave a long sigh that made her sound old and anything but happy.

For the first time, Anthony took a really good look at her. Patches of pink scalp showed through her limp, blond hair. And she was so skinny she sagged. He glanced back to the photograph of his mother, his pretty, smiling mother, and, for a moment, resentment welled up inside him. His mother was beautiful, and she was dead. Mrs. Diamond was homely, but she was alive. The lump felt bigger than ever.

"Well, I guess we'd just better get ourselves downstairs now," Mrs. Diamond said. "Mr. Diamond will want to have a talk with you. My, oh, my, you just don't know how happy he's going to be to have a boy in this house. Yes, indeed, he's just going to be sooo happy." Anthony could almost sense a note of strain in her gushy, overworked enthusiasm, especially when she added, "Mr. Diamond's always wanted a boy in the house, you know."

No, Anthony didn't know. Nor did he much care. He followed Mrs. Diamond out to a kind of bedroom balcony and down a long staircase to a good-sized hall. The house looked bigger and neater than anything he had ever lived in before, but it also looked older and shabbier. As he trailed Mrs. Diamond across the hall, he could hear the sound of television coming from a room at the back. Then the front door swung open and a girl came racing in.

"Hildy Diamond, about time you got home," Mrs. Diamond said in disapproving but hushed tones. "Another few minutes and you wouldn't have got any supper."

Hildy gave a defiant shrug. She was long and squinty,

Anthony thought, long blond hair, long face, long arms and legs. And everything about her—eyes, lips, maybe even her nose—seemed to squint.

As she tried to slip by, Mrs. Diamond said, "Hildy, you come here and say hello to your new foster brother. You two get acquainted while I go see if Mr. Diamond's ready for you, Anthony." She disappeared through a closed door off the hall.

Hildy walked over to Anthony and stared at him with hostile eyes. After a moment, she opened a mouth full of lots of dark-looking metal and said, "What's your name?"

They had met only briefly before, but surely she must remember his name. "Anthony," he said.

"Anthony what?"

"Anthony Lang, Junior."

"Junior? JUNIOR?" Hildy began to laugh as if there were something very funny about that. Anthony could feel himself bristle. When she finally stopped laughing, she said, "How old are you?"

"Eleven."

"ELEVEN? *I'm* eleven." She sounded as if no one else had the right to be eleven except her. She walked closer to him, drew herself up to her full height, put her hand on top of her head, then moved it across at the same level to hold over his head. From the first, Anthony hadn't felt sure he would like her. When she said, "For eleven, you're sure a shrimp," he knew he hated her.

Sure, he was short for his age. No one had to remind him. But it wouldn't last forever. He was going to be just like his dad. If he'd heard his dad say it once, he'd heard it a hundred times, "All of a sudden, I just shot up." And his dad was plenty tall now. Plenty tall. Before he could make a nasty reply to Hildy, she spat, "And no shrimp is going to be any brother of mine," and tore off toward the sound of television at the back of the hall. Anthony, face red with anger, glared after her.

At that moment, Mrs. Diamond appeared from behind the closed door. "You go right in, Anthony." She smiled her toothy smile again. "You and Mr. Diamond just have yourselves a nice man-to-man talk." She stood aside and Anthony timidly entered a living room as shabby and as neat as the rest of the house. Behind him, the door closed with a hollow sound.

"Come in, come in." Mr. Diamond sat on the couch. He looked up from a sheet of paper that rested on his lap. "As we used to say in the Navy, welcome aboard." He motioned toward a chair that faced the couch. "Have a seat, fella."

Anthony sat down and waited while Mr. Diamond took another look at the paper. Reading upside down, Anthony could just make out his name. Undoubtedly the agency had sent along his history.

Although Anthony had met Mr. and Mrs. Diamond several times before, and although Ms. Honeycott, the caseworker, had taken him to their house for a long visit, he felt as if he were seeing everything for the first time. But then, he had tried to avoid staring on those other occasions.

When Mr. Diamond glanced up from the paper, Anthony was a little startled to find the enormous round eyes of an owl examining him. In a moment he realized it was only Mr. Diamond's glasses magnifying his eyes. Anthony had never seen anything quite like it before. Owl eyes in a face as long and droopy as a spaniel's. They made him feel uncomfortable.

The owl eyes turned back to the paper. "Anthony Lang, Junior," the man mused. "Well, we'll have to do something about that right now, won't we?"

Do something? Anthony didn't understand.

The owl eyes fixed on him again. "Anybody call you Tony?"

"No, nobody."

"Good. Nothing like a fresh start. We'll call you Tony—nothing sissy about Tony—a real boy's name. And that Junior—no Seniors around here—we'll just drop that."

We? How did Mr. Diamond figure "we"? It was Anthony's Junior, nobody else's.

"Yes, sir—Tony Lang—new beginning, new name. What do you think of that?"

A fair question. Anthony thought and decided he didn't think much of it. When he opened his mouth to say so, Mr. Diamond said, "Well, that's settled. First things first, Tony. Might as well get our ship in order right away. You know, some people will tell you cleanliness is next to godliness. Know what I always say?"

Anthony shook his head.

"I say order is next to godliness. After all, you can't clean a counter until you get rid of all the junk on top—right?"

Anthony opened his mouth.

"Right," Mr. Diamond said. "After all, where would I be as parts manager at Willoughby Motors if I didn't believe in order?"

Anthony didn't bother to open his mouth this time.

"Straight out the door, that's where I'd be. You remember that, Tony. Order is next to godliness. First things first. Which reminds me, now that we're on names, you're probably wondering what to call *us*. Right?"

This time Anthony got out a word. "I—"

"Right. While you're in this house, Tony, you're the same as my own child. You'll call us what Hildy calls us."

Already a victim of the kind of names Hildy called people, Anthony wondered what was coming.

"You'll call the wife Mom, just like Hildy does, and me Dad."

Somewhere inside Anthony a door shut and locked. He didn't mind calling Mrs. Diamond *Mom*, because he had always called his own mother *Honey*, the way his father had. But *Dad*, that was something else. No one but his father would he ever call *Dad*. Never, never, never.

"One other thing—now I want to make this perfectly clear—while you live under my roof—and I hope that's going to be a long time, Tony—you're the same as my own son. You do your share of work, same as the rest of us, eat the same food we eat, get the same allowance Hildy gets—and no backtalk. Anything I don't put up with is a lot of backtalk. You just keep your nose clean and mind the rules of the house and we'll get along fine."

Then Mr. Diamond relaxed back on the couch and smiled at Anthony. "I tell you, Tony, I'm mighty glad to see another fella in this house. A man gets pretty sick of a whole house full of women. There's Mom and Hildy and Mom's Ma, old lady Puckett—I tell you, just too many women. A man needs another fella around. After all, how can you take a woman to a ball game? Right?"

Anthony wasn't sure about that.

"Right. Now you and me, we're going to have us some good times, Tony. Ever been to Dodger Stadium?"

"No."

"Oh, ho—have you got a treat in store for you. We'll take in some of the games this year, just the two of us. I tell you, Tony, I never been sorry I left Missour-ah."

Anthony wondered if he meant Missouri.

"No, sir, never been sorry I came to good old Torrance, California, the All-American City. Back in the part of Missour-ah I come from, you don't find anything

like Dodger Stadium less than an hour away. No, sir."
A buddy-to-buddy smile spread over Mr. Diamond's
face. "How's your pitching arm, fella?"

Anthony shrugged. "Not too good, I guess."

"Well, we'll have to do something about that, won't
we?"

Anthony looked down at his arms resting rigidly on
the chair and wondered what kind of something Mr.
Diamond had in mind.

"Well, I guess that's about all for now. About time
you and me washed up for supper, Tony." Mr. Diamond got to his feet. Anthony stood up, too, noticing
that the man was shorter than his father. Anthony was
awfully glad he wasn't Mr. Diamond's son. Then he
would have had no hope of ever shooting up.

"Tell you what, Tony. Tonight you get to say grace at
the table. Nothing like starting you off on the good
road. Right?"

Wrong. As Anthony followed Mr. Diamond out of
the living room, he decided "Grace" must be somebody's name. Mrs. Diamond's, probably. He also decided it would be a lot easier to say Grace than Mom.

2

They Keep Us Alive for the Money

Long after supper was over, long after the house lay in darkness, long after the sound of the television set ceased to issue from the room at the back of the downstairs hall, Anthony tossed restlessly on his bed. Every time he thought of the word *grace*, he squirmed.

After Mr. Diamond had told the family Anthony's new name, he'd said, "Well, Tony, how about it? You ready to say grace?"

Anthony looked around the table. Mrs. Diamond gave him her toothy smile, Hildy, her mean squint. It seemed pretty silly to Anthony, but if that was what Mr. Diamond wanted, he figured he'd better say it. He looked at Mrs. Diamond and said, "Grace . . . ?" Then he wondered if maybe he should have said, "Hi, Grace." He glanced at Mr. Diamond. The owl eyes transfixed him.

"You trying to be funny, fella? If there's one thing we

don't stand for around here, it's irreverence for the Lord. No, sir."

Anthony's stomach went all tight. He had done something wrong. And somehow he didn't think a "Hi, Grace" would improve matters. He turned to Mrs. Diamond, a frightened and bewildered look on his face.

"He doesn't know what you mean, Ed," she said to her husband. Then she gave Anthony a sympathetic smile. "I'll just bet you've never been around people who said grace."

No, Anthony hadn't. Too frightened to speak, he shook his head.

"There, you see, Ed—you can't blame the boy for never hearing anybody say grace."

Mr. Diamond pondered that strange possibility for a moment. "That right, Tony?"

Right. Anthony nodded.

Hildy gave him a snide grin. Then, looking sanctimonious and smug, she said, "I can say it, Dad."

"Never mind, Hildy."

"But I know how—"

"I said, never mind."

"But, Dad, I can say it real good. Just the other day I—"

"Shut up, Hildy." Mr. Diamond's voice was sharply impatient. Hildy sank back in her chair with a scowl.

Anthony felt a secret stab of satisfaction. He would have enjoyed telling Hildy to shut up himself.

"Now, Tony," Mr. Diamond said, "you just listen to

me real good. When I'm not here for dinner, I expect you to be the man of the family and say grace."

Anthony listened real good as Mr. Diamond thanked the Lord, at length, for bountiful food, for everyone's good health, for a comfortable home, for countless other blessings, and, last but not least, for the boy, Tony Lang, entrusted to Mr. Diamond's care to be raised in the paths of righteousness, and of the Lord, amen.

Now, as he lay sleepless on his bed, Anthony gave a long sigh. He wished he could grow up with his dad instead of in the paths of righteousness and of a Lord who was starting to look more and more like Mr. Diamond. The empty-hungry feeling began to fill him again like a balloon near bursting. He missed his father. He missed the Sauters who were friends of his father's. And he very much missed his own name. Now he was Tony Lang, whoever that was. Nobody. Tears began to trickle down his cheeks.

It was a long time before they stopped. He lay there, still sleepless, for what seemed like hours, his mouth feeling as parched and burny as his eyes. He longed for a glass of water but was afraid that if he used the upstairs bathroom, someone might hear him. Finally he decided to tiptoe down to the kitchen.

Out in the hall a night light cast a dim glow along the staircase. Worn carpeting muffled his steps. A street light shone through narrow glass insets beside the front door and guided him along the corridor to the kitchen. He slipped inside the door, grateful to see moonlight streaming through the windows, dimly showing the way to the sink. Not daring to risk the noise of opening and closing cabinets, he carefully turned the tap until a gentle stream of water issued from it. He cupped his hands and drank until his thirst was quenched. Then he turned off the tap, dried his mouth on the back of his hand, and started back the way he had come.

He had taken only a few steps when, someplace, a floorboard creaked. Anthony froze. In the next instant a click sounded and light flooded the room. He found himself staring at a tiny old woman in a nightgown. She looked as surprised as he. The next thing he knew, she was shuffling over to him with the help of a cane, her face contorted as if every movement gave her pain. She peered down into his face, opened a toothless mouth, and, in a crochety voice, said, "What you up to, boy, sneaking around in the dark? You aiming to steal something?"

She must think him a burglar. "I—I was just getting a drink of water." Surely she must be the old woman Mr. Diamond mentioned. What was it he'd called her? Old lady Puckett. Anthony remembered Mrs. Diamond had taken a tray someplace at suppertime.

The old woman continued staring at him in a way that made him think she was trying to decide who he was. "I live here now," he said. "Didn't anyone tell you?"

Instead of answering, her eyes rested on his face in a

fixed stare. Was she looking at him or right through him? He began to feel uncomfortable. When he repeated the question, she blinked, apparently trying to get him into focus.

"Eh?" she said.

"Didn't Mr. and Mrs. Diamond tell you I've come to live here?"

"Come to live here?" she said, her voice sounding foggy. She shook her head. "I disremember." Then she turned from him and started toward the refrigerator. Suddenly she stopped, twisted her neck slightly, and talked over her shoulder. "You the foster boy?"

Then they *had* told her. "Yes."

"Humph," was all she had to say to that. She continued on to the refrigerator, muttering to herself, "Sneaking around in the dark—up to no good—burglars and dope fiends, that's all any of them are these days. Can't trust them in your house."

Anthony was surprised to realize she was talking about him. "I wasn't sneaking. Honest. I couldn't sleep, and I didn't want to wake anybody. I just wanted a drink of water."

"Humph!" She opened the refrigerator and pulled out something that looked like a milk carton. She took a pan from a lower cupboard and poured in the contents of the container. "Long as you're here, put this on the stove for me. This'll help the both of us sleep."

Anthony put the pan on the stove and turned on the

burner underneath. "I guess I'd better get back to bed now."

The old woman ignored the words. She pointed to an upper cupboard. "Get some cups and saucers."

Not knowing what else to do, Anthony obeyed her. He set the cups and saucers on the kitchen table. Then she pointed to a chair. "Sit down."

Anthony sat down.

She settled herself in the chair opposite his, and they both waited in silence. After a long time, she said, "You better look at that milk. Don't let it boil. It ain't ready until there's scum on top."

Anthony got up and looked into the pan. He could see something that looked like wrinkled skin over the surface. "I guess it's ready."

"Fill the cups."

He turned off the gas and poured the steaming liquid into the cups. Scum or skin, either one sounded unappetizing. The old woman sipped hers. Anthony stared at his.

"Well, drink it," she said. "You want to sleep, don't you?"

Reluctantly, he picked up the cup. Never in his life had he drunk hot milk. The strange warm smell of it made him unconsciously wrinkle his nose.

"Oh, you think you're being poisoned, do you? That's goat's milk, boy. No poison in that. It's cow's milk that'll do you in."

Goat's milk? Anthony's stomach lurched.

"Drink it, boy —make you sleep like a baby, and you ain't far from that."

Anthony took a cautious sip and almost gagged. He was going to put down the cup, but he saw the old woman's eyes on him, so he gulped a little more. Perhaps if he finished it off quickly he wouldn't taste it so much.

"No, boy, nobody's going to poison you in this house. You know why?"

Anthony shook his head, a little uneasy at all that talk of poison.

She leaned over and, with a bony, misshapen finger, poked him in the chest. "Because you're too valuable."

"Valuable?"

With the air of someone sharing a great secret, she leaned even closer to him. Instinctively, he drew back. "Oh, yes, boy, we're both too valuable," she said in a whisper. Then she looked over her shoulder, apparently making sure no one was listening at the door. She turned back to him and, in a normal tone, said, "Oh, no, no poison. They want to keep us alive."

Anthony squirmed in his chair. "They do?"

"Oh, yes—for the money—my pension and whatever they get for you. That's all *they* care about. They've kept me prisoner in this house for years. Now it's your turn, boy."

A shiver ran up Anthony's spine.

The old woman reached over and grasped his arm. Like claws, her nails dug in. In an urgent voice, she said, "You've got to get a letter to my son, Edgar Doyle Puckett. And don't you say a word about it to nobody, y'hear?"

Anthony, his eyes wide, nodded.

"Edgar Doyle would like to know how they treat me around here. Oh, yes. He'd be here in a minute and yank me out of this hell. I'd have a good life with Edgar Doyle." The claws loosened on Anthony's arm, and the old woman slumped back into her chair. Her eyes glazed over. In a vague and wistful voice, she said, "Edgar Doyle used to bring me chocolates and pretty pink and green mints. 'For my best girl,' he'd say. He treated me like a queen. Oh, yes, I'd have a good life with Edgar Doyle." She gave a deep sigh. Then her eyes cleared and flicked back to Anthony. "Drink up, boy. You want to sleep, don't you?"

Somehow Anthony got down the rest of his milk. Then he delicately sidled out of his chair, unmindful of his dirty cup and saucer, hoping only that she would let him go. "I guess I'd better get to bed now," he said and began to edge toward the door. The old woman paid him no attention. She picked up her cup and again began to sip. Anthony fled from the room.

Swiftly and quietly, he made his way back to bed to creep under the safety of the covers. The old woman's words, all mixed up, kept ringing in his ears. Poison . . . cow's milk will do you in for the money . . . poison goat's milk . . . make you sleep like a prisoner. Anthony shuddered. She must be crazy.

Thoroughly unnerved by the episode in the kitchen, he thought he would be awake all night. But soon the milk began warming his stomach, relaxing him. After a time, he drifted into a troubled sleep.

3

Keeping in Touch
with Reality

Ms. Honeycott sat behind her desk and smiled at Anthony. Under other circumstances he believed he might have liked her. In his present situation, he felt she had done him a great wrong. He scrutinized her carefully for evidence of guilt. But, no, she kept her treachery hidden behind two true-blue eyes and a face that registered only countless sterling qualities.

Something else about Ms. Honeycott. She had a boyfriend. If you got her talking about him, sometimes you didn't hear a lot of other things you didn't want to hear.

"How's your boyfriend?" Anthony said.

She gave a nice tinkly laugh. "Oh, no, you don't—I'm onto that trick now. We're not here to talk about me. How about you? Getting used to your new home after your first week?"

For some reason Anthony couldn't come right out and tell her how much he hated it and how much he blamed her for his plight. Yet he wanted her to know and choke on the guilt. "I think I'll go back with the Sauters."

"Oh, Anthony— You know you can't do that. We've been all over it."

Yes, Anthony knew. There was the new baby, the Sauters' move to Lancaster, the smaller house. And worse, the board money his father had promised them when he'd left Anthony there eight months before. None of it had come. Then, at long last, the phone call from his dad. Mr. Sauter saying, "We'd like to keep the boy, but we can't. We've got four kids of our own now. We just don't have the room."

Then more talk back and forth, something about turning it over to an agency. And all the while, Anthony standing by, eagerly waiting to speak to his dad. Finally, Mr. Sauter saying, "If there's no alternative, that's what we're going to do. We've made up our minds." After that, his dad's voice explaining to Anthony that it would be only for a little while, only until he got settled.

Now here Anthony was, sitting in an agency, trying to understand the tempest that had blown into his life and landed him with the Diamonds. "Did you hear from my dad yet?" he asked.

"No, we didn't, Anthony."

"Well, I guess it won't be long. He ought to get settled any day now. Then we'll get a house and a housekeeper. It'll be like old times."

He could see Ms. Honeycott's life-is-for-real look

transform her face. "Anthony, you must try to realize that all that may never happen. Parents often feel guilty when they can't take care of their children. Sometimes they make a lot of promises they can't keep. As long as your father doesn't have a job, he can't take care of you."

"He'll get a job. He's an aeronautical engineer!"

"It's not as simple as that. Your dad had several rather earthshaking experiences. First, he lost the good job he'd had for so many years. Then there was your mother's illness and death, and all the financial problems, hospital bills and other kinds—and having to sell the house to pay them. According to what the Sauters have told us, your dad just couldn't seem to recover from all those hard blows. Some people never do, Anthony—even nice people like your father."

What was she trying to tell him? That his dad was finished? "My dad will be okay just as soon as he gets another job," he said stoutly.

"As far as we know, your father hasn't worked in over four years. That's a long time. And now, more and more people are out of work. It's harder than ever to get a job."

"My dad will."

"Anthony, we haven't heard a word from your father. We don't even know where he is. Remember what I told you—we all have to keep in touch with reality."

"Oh, sure," Anthony said. Ms. Honeycott was very big on reality. Her trouble was, she couldn't seem to realize that as soon as his dad was settled, everything would be all right. That was reality.

To his relief, she changed the subject. "Well, tell me about your week."

But there were no words to tell anyone anything about that miserable week. What words could ever make somebody understand that big lump inside him? Instead, all he could do was play a little game with her, a game called, Tell Them Everything But What They Want to Hear. After all, wasn't that what she did with him? All you had to do, he'd found out, was say something, then watch those true-blues. One blink and you knew you'd set off a ground tremor, two, a decided shock, and three—well, he had never accomplished that yet, but he was sure three would have been an earthquake, maybe even a 7.5er on the Richter scale.

Glancing at her out of the corner of an eye, he said, "All the Diamonds want is the money they get for having me live with them."

Not a blink, not even a flutter.

"Oh, Anthony, that's not true. Often foster parents couldn't afford to take in children without some financial help, but that isn't the reason they do it. Besides, do you think any amount of money would be worth all the problems they face?"

"I'm not a problem."

"No, but some young people are."

Anthony shrugged. Again he kept watch out of the corner of his eyes. "The old lady's crazy."

Only a ground tremor.

"I know she's a little senile. Some old people are. We just have to understand and be patient."

"What's senile mean?" Anthony asked.

"It means that, at times, she's out of touch with reality."

There was that old reality again. He said, "She keeps her television on all day and all night, and she doesn't even look at it."

"Perhaps she feels less lonely with it on."

"She drinks goat's milk, too."

A one blinker.

"Goat's milk?"

"Mr. Diamond has to go out of his way to a special dairy to pick it up after work. One night he forgot and she told him if she didn't have her goat's milk, she'd die, sure as God made green apples, and what would he do without her pension money then? Mr. Diamond about blew his top."

"Well, old people are sometimes difficult to live with, Anthony. I suppose any of us might get impatient with them at times. But we get impatient with all people, young or old. It's part of life. Anything else on your mind?"

"Yes."

"Tell me."

"He wants me to play baseball."

"Something wrong with that?"

"My dad never liked baseball. He liked car races and air shows."

"That doesn't mean you have to restrict yourself to those. Everything we do enriches our lives."

"Yeah, but he's talking Little League."

"Well, it just might be fun. Lots of boys *do* enjoy it."

"Not me."

"How do you know if you haven't tried?"

"I just know."

Ms. Honeycott refused to pursue the subject. Instead she said, "How's your new school?"

Annoyed that she was turning the conversation away from the Diamonds and heading it down on her own road, he gave an indifferent shrug, then cut himself off from her by staring up at the ceiling and counting the black holes in the accoustical tiles.

At length she said, "Something else on your mind?"

He took his time before glancing back to her. Disgruntled that he wasn't getting through in the way he'd hoped, he thought for a moment, then said, "I just might run away."

Two delicate blinks this time. Not a decided shock, but close.

Very seriously, she said, "Where to?"

"I'll think of someplace."

"How will you support yourself?"

"I'll think of something."

Ms. Honeycott gave him a you're-being-very-silly-but-I-like-you-anyhow smile. "Remember what I said about reality?"

Anthony might have expected that. It must have been all of five minutes since they'd been in touch with reality.

"Anthony, changes are hard to make. It takes a while to get used to new situations, new demands. But it will all come right in the end, you'll see."

But Anthony didn't see, at least not in her way. Yet he found himself saying, "How do you know it will?"

"Because, one way or another, it usually does."

It was the one way or another that disturbed him.

Finally Ms. Honeycott said, "Mrs. Diamond will be waiting for you now," and Anthony knew their talk was over. The caseworker set up another appointment for him, marking it carefully on her desk calendar. Then she walked with him to the door.

Before they joined Mrs. Diamond outside, Anthony took one more stab at the true-blues. "If I don't run away, I just might kill that Hildy."

Two good blinks!

It took her a moment before she said, "Aw—" in a voice that good-naturedly chided him for teasing her, then roughed his hair playfully.

"Tell me about your week." Oh, sure. Tell her about how Mr. Diamond came home from work a little before dark each night and said, "Come on, Tony, let's toss a few," and about how impatient the man was every time

Anthony missed the ball? Tell her about how Anthony hated the whole thing, dreaded to see Mr. Diamond walk in the door? Tell her about the big wire fence that Mr. Diamond had worked on over the weekend? The same fence that, to Anthony's surprise, now stood finished and waiting as he and Mrs. Diamond returned home.

"Well, it's all yours, Tony," Mr. Diamond said. "I took off from work early and finished it. Now as soon as you get in from school every day, you get out here and practice for all you're worth. You want to be ready for those try-outs in a couple of weeks."

Anthony looked at the special area for batting and pitching, an area that took in most of the yard, and wished he were dead.

"And look what else you've got." Mr. Diamond, who was already wearing one, tossed a catcher's mitt to Anthony. "Put it on." He strode over to the porch where Hildy stood, amusing herself swinging a bat. "Gimme that, Hildy." He took the bat from her hands and turned it over to Anthony. "How about that? Brand new."

Anthony could see it was. Mrs. Diamond stood beside him, showing every gleaming tooth in her head. "My, isn't that nice," she said. "Just like Christmas."

Anthony gave a weak smile. "Yeah."

"Well, come on, Tony, let's see if this thing is going to work."

Mrs. Diamond went into the house to fix supper. Hildy sat down on the porch steps to watch. Mr. Diamond, a big grin on his face, jokingly yelled, "Play ball!"

"What do you want me to do?" Anthony said glumly.

"Come here. I'll show you." Mr. Diamond walked to the back of the fenced area. For the first time, Anthony noticed a big piece of plywood sitting up on a stand. Mr. Diamond pointed to a hole in the wood. "The object is to throw the ball through here. I read about this someplace—helps you work on coordination and control."

Anthony placed the bat well behind him on the grass. Then Mr. Diamond tossed him a ball and moved out of the way. "Let's see what you can do," he said.

Anthony reluctantly backed up. To him, the hole looked about the size of a pea. He took aim, threw, and hit the wire fence instead of the plywood.

Mr. Diamond said crossly, "You missed by a mile. Can't you do any better than that?"

From time to time, Anthony had played baseball in school or with some of the guys in somebody's yard. But that was just fooling around. This was something else. If he had never taken much interest in the game before, tossing balls at a hole in a piece of wood made him surer than ever that he'd never make a baseball player. It was Mr. Diamond, not Anthony, who needed to keep in touch with reality.

Once more Anthony stepped back and took aim. A dud. He tried again. And again. And again. He must have taken a dozen shots at that hole, but not one came close.

"I bet I could do it, Dad," Hildy said in her usual maddening way.

"Never mind, Hildy."

"I pitched a whole game in school yesterday."

"Hildy, shut up. Can't you find something else to do—go in the house and help your mother or something. You're making Tony nervous."

"She can't make *me* nervous," Anthony said. She could, and she did, but he wasn't about to admit it.

"Well, she makes me nervous." Mr. Diamond glowered at her and Hildy fell silent. He turned back to Anthony. "That's enough with the board. You practice those shots every day until you get that ball through every time. Now we'll try a little batting."

Anthony picked up the gleaming bat, already feeling that the session would never end. Mr. Diamond told him where and how to stand and what grip to use. All the while, Anthony could feel the stab of Hildy's eyes.

"Used to do quite a bit of pitching in my day." Mr. Diamond walked as far from Anthony as the yard allowed. He turned around, plopped the ball in his gloved fist a couple of times and asked, "You ready?"

Anthony shifted uncomfortably, gripped the bat hard and nodded. Mr. Diamond hunched his shoulders, then began the wind-up. In the next instant, a rocket shot toward Anthony. He jumped back as if it might bite him. The rocket hit the fence, then rolled back toward him. He heard Hildy giggle, and his face reddened. When her father glanced sharply at her, she clasped her palm over her mouth, muffling the sound, but her shoulders shook with silent laughter.

"You're chickening out, Tony," Mr. Diamond said. "Let's try it again."

Anthony picked up the ball and tossed it back. On the second try, Anthony again hopped back. This time, Hildy laughed out loud, but her father was too annoyed with Anthony to notice. "Come on, now," he said. "That was a good clean pitch. Take it. You want to get into Little League, don't you?"

No, Anthony didn't. The whole idea had come from Mr. Diamond. Now, suddenly, it was supposed to be Anthony's. Things could sure get turned all around, he thought. As he got into position again, a movement from Hildy caught his attention. She was getting to her feet. Apparently she realized Anthony but not her father could see her. She stretched out her arms and pointed both thumbs toward the ground.

Anthony tore his eyes from her. A blinding rage swept through him. She was doing everything she could think of to put him off. He watched Mr. Diamond who was winding up again. At the instant the ball left her father's hand, Hildy, as if compelled, shrieked, "Throw the bum out!"

When the ball came zooming toward Anthony, it had Hildy's face stamped all over it. No jumping back this time. Anthony swung and smacked it with a force that surprised even him. The ball sailed up, up, up and over the fence. He stood there, mouth open, watching it head for the building across the street, a church annex. In another second, the sound of shattering glass cut through him like the agonizing pain of a mortal wound. All he could do was stand there and wish someone would finish him off before Mr. Diamond got to him. Which, from the look of it, wouldn't be long. He could see the flush of anger on the man's face, the sparks that almost seemed to shoot from those enormous eyes.

Mr. Diamond looked from Anthony to Hildy, over to the church annex, back to Anthony, back to Hildy, as if torn between which deserved the sting of his wrath. In the next moment, he tore over to Hildy. She took a quick fearful glance toward the back door, obviously measuring her chances to run. Before she could move, Mr. Diamond grabbed the collar of her pullover and held her fast. The sound of the slap across her face rang through the yard. Hildy's hand shot to her cheek as she tried to shrink away. Mr. Diamond hung on. "You get your behind in the house and on up to your room. And you stay there until I tell you to come out, y'hear?"

Tears glistened like shiny beads in her eyes as she nodded.

"And don't you let me catch you out here during practice again." He released her with a shove. "Now git."

Hildy, still holding her cheek, turned and fled

through the back door. Mr. Diamond stared after her for a moment, then swung around and marched over to Anthony. Anthony held his breath. In another moment, the man's face began to relax as some of the anger drained from it. Anthony slowly breathed out.

"I have to say—you can sure hit when you want to. But while you're in the yard, you take it easy. Don't swing so hard. Understand?"

Feeling relieved and bewildered at the same time, Anthony nodded. It was he who'd broken the window, yet Mr. Diamond had punished Hildy. Not that she didn't deserve it, calling him a bum that way.

"Well, now I'll have to phone the church and tell them what you done." Mr. Diamond looked annoyed at the thought. "And the money to fix that window comes out of your allowance. We all got to learn to take responsibility for our actions. Now go clean up for supper."

Anthony took the bat and mitt with him into the house. Mr. Diamond followed, heading toward the kitchen. "Might make a baseball player out of you yet."

Anthony attempted a smile, but, inside, he felt a little sick. Then he hurried through the house to the hall. To his surprise, he found Hildy waiting for him at the foot of the staircase.

She glared at him. "I HATE YOU! I wish you'd die." Before he could answer, she whipped around and ran up the stairs toward her room.

4

Nobody Wants a Shrimp on Their Team

For the next two weeks, Anthony felt as if he had somehow landed in the middle of a bad dream. Each day he put in his time in school but found it difficult to interest himself in anything there. What was the use anyhow? He knew he'd be gone as soon as his father was settled. He kept to himself, not bothering to try to make friends, not paying much attention to the work or the activities, grateful only that he was in a different room from Hildy's.

He had still another blessing. And one for which he would have enjoyed thanking the Lord when he had to stammer through grace at dinner. He walked to and from school alone. Hildy always ran on ahead to poke her way into some group of girls. Anthony noticed they seemed to enjoy her company about as much as he did. He also noticed that no matter how many times her father sat on her, Hildy bounced right back for more, never knowing when to shut up, always making herself as obnoxious as possible.

After school each day Anthony went through the motions of practicing out in the backyard. When Mr. Diamond joined him later, it was always the same old thing, hit harder, not so hard, too much swing, not enough. When dinner was over, Anthony would sit in his room and catch up on homework or work on his model airplane. Then there were the visits to Ms. Honeycott's office. And on Sundays, of course, it was church. Nothing he did seemed real. He went through the days feeling nothing.

At home, the old woman was a shadowy presence, yet she managed to keep Mrs. Diamond hopping with her constant demands. She would poke her head out of her room or come shuffling through the house, always looking for Margie, always complaining. Margie knew right well she was supposed to give her mother a massage, or a hot water bottle, or pick up medicine from the drug store. A body could die and who'd care? Not Margie. She cared more about taking in dope fiends off the street than tending her own mother. She'd be sorry. Oh, yes, sure as God made green apples, she'd be sorry when there was no more pension money. Anthony always felt uneasy around her, and tried to avoid her as much as possible.

On the Friday night before the Little League try-outs, he kept to his room after dinner. He worked on his P–51 model, but his mind was on the following day. If he

didn't make a good showing, Mr. Diamond would blow
his top. If he did make a good showing, he was stuck
with baseball.

He finally realized that with all his fidgeting he was
doing his model more harm than good, so he put it
down. Mrs. Diamond had given him permission to help
himself to snacks from a special shelf in the refrigerator.
He decided to see if she had put in any soft drinks.

He went downstairs to the kitchen only to discover he
had chosen the wrong moment. Old Mrs. Puckett was
there, pouring some of her hot goat's milk into a cup.
Before he could scoot out, she spotted him. "Come
here, boy," she said, beckoning him toward the table.
Reluctantly, Anthony walked over.

She motioned toward a chair. "Sit down." As he sat
down, she shoved the full cup under his nose, then took
another from the cupboard and filled it for herself.
"Now you sit right there, boy. If anybody comes in,
you're just having a cup of hot milk with me." She
glanced toward the service porch off the kitchen.
Beyond it, Mr. Diamond had closed in a former patio to
make a family room. Anthony could hear music coming
from the big, color television set out there.

The old woman sat down facing him, all the time
keeping an eye on the service porch. Anthony, not sure
of how mentally unstable she was, took some comfort
from the thought that others in the family were close by.
She glanced at him impatiently. "Well, drink up, drink
up."

Not again! He silently groaned. This time he made short work of the rotten stuff, gulping it down all at once. Anything to get away from her. When he started to rise, she waved him back into his chair. Then she reached into the pocket of a worn flannel bathrobe and drew out an envelope so crumpled it looked as if she had carried it around for days. "Here, boy," she said, thrusting it into his hands. "You mail this for me. And don't you tell nobody, y'hear?"

Anthony glanced at it to see she had addressed it to Edgar Doyle Puckett in some place in New Mexico, no street address. At least she had remembered the stamp.

"Now you go put that in the box up to the corner. And you hear what I told you? Not a word to nobody."

"I won't say anything," he said and left the room as fast as he could. He slipped out the front door, walked to the corner mailbox, got rid of the letter, then made his way back to the house and up to his bedroom. If the old woman wanted to write to her son, why shouldn't she? And if she thought she had to make a big secret out of it, what did he care? Or anyone else, for that matter? He went out to the bathroom and brushed his teeth to get the taste of goat's milk out of his mouth.

Anthony, number 137 on his back, lined up with the other eleven-year-olds, waiting his turn for base runs. One part of his mind was aware of all the activity around him, of the Diamonds in the bleachers, of the man outside the high chain-link fence writing down an assessment of each boy's performance. Another part of Anthony's mind was so busy worrying about how he would do, he only dimly heard someone call, "Next boy."

"Hey, you asleep or something?" The boy behind him gave Anthony a shove. The jolt brought him to life. As the others ahead of him had done, he ran over to home base.

"What's your name?" a man with a stopwatch asked. When Anthony told him, he yelled out to the keeper of the books, "This is Tony Lang," then said to Anthony, "Okay, Tony."

Anthony crouched in position.

". . . ready . . . get set . . . GO!"

Anthony ran as fast as he could to first base, then on toward second. The diamond had looked small to him before. Now as he hit second and started toward third, he was certain the field was growing. Third base, at last. Finally, home.

Loud enough for everyone to hear, the man with the stopwatch said, "Ten seconds."

Anthony knew the other boys were making it in about eight seconds. As he started to head back toward the sidelines, Stopwatch said, "Wait a minute, Tony. You sure you're in the right group?"

"Yessir."

"How old are you?"

"Eleven."

"Eleven, huh? Well, okay."

Dismissed. Anthony walked back to the other boys, feeling deeply humiliated.

"What was that all about?" one of the kids asked.

Anthony shrugged although he knew very well "what was that all about." He was shorter and slower than any kid in the try-outs. Stopwatch undoubtedly thought he belonged with the younger boys.

Fielding trials came next. Some of the boys made good showings, but not Anthony. Wearing one of the helmets someone had provided, he stood out on the field, trying to catch grounders and fly balls and throw them to first base. Everything seemed to get by him. And half the time, he threw short of the boy on first, an older boy who was there only to help out. With each miss, Anthony visualized the man outside the fence writing in that big book, *lousy, super lousy, throw the bum out!*

Afterward he heard one of the real hot-shots saying to another kid, "Wow, even an eight-year-old could do better than that." Anthony knew they were talking about him. Hearing that really great praise was bad enough, but, even worse, he could just imagine what Mr. Diamond was saying up there in the bleachers. And he didn't have to imagine what Hildy was saying. Well, who cared? None of this was his idea anyhow.

When the last boy had had his turn on the field, everyone lined up for batting. Stopwatch acted as pitcher, another man as catcher. Each boy had to hit about a half-dozen balls. When Anthony's turn came, he walked dejectedly up to the batter's box. The kid who'd just finished passed the bat to him. Anthony noticed it felt somewhat lighter than the one he had at home. He took his position in the box and waited. As pitcher and catcher talked back and forth for a moment, Anthony rearranged dirt with his sneakers.

Finally Stopwatch said, "You ready, Tony?"

Anthony, feeling tense, gripped the bat tight and gave a quick bob of his head.

The pitcher began winding up. Only too conscious of all the eyes turned on him now, Anthony shifted uncomfortably. In the next instant, the ball whizzed toward his head. Or so it seemed. He leaped out of the way. Immediately laughter rang out from the sidelines. Blood crept up to his face and settled there. While the catcher returned the ball to the pitcher, Anthony took a quick glance behind home base to see the keeper of the books write down something. *Chicken!* In the book or not, Anthony could feel the word emblazoned in blood across his forehead.

Stopwatch was again winding up. Again the ball surprised Anthony, coming at him like something shot from a cannon. And again he jumped back. More laughter. *Double chicken!* Although the day was cold and damp, his palms felt all sweaty. He wiped them on his jeans and glanced toward the bleachers, eyes fastening on Hildy long enough to see her hand clapped across her mouth. He knew what that meant. He'd thought nothing and no one could get to him these

days. But Hildy could and did. Now anger burned inside him. He was so mad at that girl, nothing else
seemed to matter.

"Tony, this time try keeping your eye on the ball,"
the pitcher said.

This time Anthony did just that. The moment the
ball left the man's hand, Anthony glued his eyes to it.
As it came toward the plate, he swung and whacked it
with all the strength in him. The ball shot high into the
air, over center field and clear out toward the fence.

"That's right," Stopwatch said. "Always keep your eye
on the ball. Don't let it surprise you."

The advice seemed to work. With each new pitch,
Anthony fixed his eyes on the ball and no longer felt
compelled to jump back. He swung and hit, swung and
hit. *Whack! Whack! Whack!* And he felt as if he could
have gone on all day.

"Good," the pitcher said, and Anthony had to pass
the bat to the next boy.

Try-outs were over for him now. As he started out the
gate to join the Diamonds, he felt a little better about
himself, almost pleased. "Good," Stopwatch had said.
Not, "Okay, next boy," as he'd said to the others. But
GOOD. It was then that the significance of the word hit
Anthony. "Good" meant he just might wind up in Little
League!

Anthony moped through the next few days. The more
he thought about it, the less he wanted anything to do

with Little League. It seemed to him that everyone was squeezing him into a corner.

Mrs. Diamond said, "You did real good, Tony. They'll be glad to get a nice boy like you."

Mr. Diamond said, "Well, your fielding's no good, and you can't throw worth a hoot, but nobody's passing up a good batter. And I got a hunch you just might be a natural. Don't worry, one of the good teams will grab you."

Yet not everyone was rooting for him. Old Mrs. Puckett couldn't have cared less. All she was interested in was sneaking more letters to him to dump in the corner mailbox. And Hildy? Nothing would have pleased her more than his failure. She caught him alone one day after school and got in her usual stab. "You'll never make it. They want guys that can do everything. You can't run and you can't throw. You can't even catch a ball. Besides, nobody wants a shrimp on their team."

The only suitable retort Anthony could come up with was, "Aw, your mother eats garbage."

"Ooooo," Hildy said, squinting her squinty little eyes poisonously. "You take that back or I'll swat you."

"You swat me, and I'll swat you right back."

Hildy glared at him, but she didn't try any swatting. Instead she said, "If anybody eats garbage, it's your father."

Now Anthony was mad. "You take that back!"

"I'm not taking anything back until you take yours

back. You started it, talking about my mother that way."

"Aw, I wasn't talking about your mother." Anthony couldn't even remember where he'd heard the expression, but he'd thought it a great one until Hildy applied it to his father. "It's just a way of talking. Don't you know anything?"

"I sure know an insult when I hear one."

Anthony sniffed. "Anybody who gives out as many as you sure ought to." He stomped off and on up to his room. For once he'd had the last word.

When he recovered from his anger, he took a pencil and a ruler from the Goodwill desk, opened his closet door, stood with his back against it and sat the ruler on his head. Holding it firm, he ducked out from under and marked the spot. His shooting up had to be due soon. He wanted to revel in every inch. And when he shot up taller than that Hildy—well, she'd just better watch out, that's all.

On that same afternoon, the devastating news came. Mrs. Diamond went up to Anthony's room to deliver the blow. "I'll just bet you can't guess what I've got to tell you," she said, smiling all over the place.

Anthony guessed all right. "What?" he asked, hoping he was wrong.

"You got into Little League! And you're going to be on a team called the Padres. That sounds to me like the very best team. Oh, I just think that's sooo nice."

Anthony gave a sick smile. "Yeah, great," he said. What else could he say?

When she left him to mull over his fate, Anthony spent the rest of the afternoon worrying. What was he doing on a baseball team anyhow? So he had hit a few lucky balls. What did that mean? Although he hated to admit it, Hildy was right. He couldn't throw, he couldn't catch, he couldn't run. He'd foul up everything. And what would his dad think? His dad had never cared for baseball.

At dinner, Little League was all anyone seemed to talk about. Except Anthony. Except Hildy. Mr. Diamond acted as if Anthony were about to go into professional baseball. Mrs. Diamond kept saying it was just sooo nice. Hildy kept trying to change the subject.

When Anthony went to bed that night, he felt sick to his stomach. If only his dad would get settled soon. He tossed and turned and thought about things. He tried to remember the early days, the good days, the time when all was right with his world. Somehow the only picture he could bring into focus was life in the apartment, a seedy place that had seemed more like a run-down motel. That was long after the house had been sold, long after his dad had stopped looking for work. Anthony could still see himself leaving for school each morning, his dad in bed. And all too often, when he returned, his dad was still in bed, lying there staring up at the ceiling. And then there were the nights. His dad would go out and come back, eyes glazed over, speech slurred. And he had the same smell about him that always drifted out of the corner beer joint when you walked past. Anthony tried to block out the picture. After all, that was all over and done with. Now his dad was really trying. Why, if he had to search through the whole country, his dad would find a job, an even better one this time.

5

Three Strikes, You're Out

"I'll tell you something, Anthony," Ms. Honeycott said. "At first I wasn't quite sure we'd made the right decision, placing you with the Diamonds. Now I have a feeling you're beginning to adapt."

That's all she knew.

She smiled at him. "Mrs. Diamond says Little League practice sessions have started. I don't know too much about baseball. What do you do at practice?"

"Oh—we play catch and stuff like that."

"What 'stuff like that'?"

Well, she was asking for it. He decided to impress her. "Oh, we practice offensive drills like hit and run and steal, or combination-sacrifice. Then we have base running and base coaching drills. And defensive relay throws, cutoffs, defense against a sacrifice. You know—all the usual stuff." From the two quick blinks of the true-blues, it was obvious she didn't know. Neither had

Anthony until recently. He added, "And of course we have lots of batting drills."

"Oh, yes—of course. I hear you're quite a batter."

"Not really." He wasn't trying to sound modest. He felt it was no credit to him that he seemed to hit straighter and harder than some of the others. "The coach says I've got a strong forearm and wrist. That's the only reason I'm better than average." Anthony had been pleased to discover that physical size had nothing to do with one's ability to cut at a ball. And to his great relief, after he'd consistently made good showings at bat, the other kids began to back off on their cracks about his poor fielding.

"Mrs. Diamond tells me Mr. Diamond is enjoying Little League as much as anybody."

"Yeah," Anthony said dismally. More than anybody, he thought. He hated most those days when Mr. Diamond came home early enough to take him to practice. The guy always had to hang around, talking to the coach or the manager, or anyone who would listen. And he always went into a blow by blow description of every game and play in which he had, single-handed, brought the opposing team to its knees. It was always the ninth inning, the other team at bat, bases loaded, two out, score tied, when Mr. Diamond marched out as relief pitcher and saved the day.

Worse than his bragging and his endless stories was his ready supply of helpful hints for the coach. Now he didn't really want to tell another guy his business, but in

Mr. Diamond's day, they'd used a different stance in the batter's box, gripped the bat a different way. And he was only too happy to demonstrate.

Even worse than Helpful Hints were Complaints. He sure didn't see why the Majors instead of the Minors hadn't bid for a kid like Tony. After all, a kid with a real batting talent didn't come along every day. In his opinion, Tony was wasted in the Minors. Anthony always felt so ashamed. He knew he wasn't that good. Now he said, "It's too bad Mr. Diamond isn't young enough to get into Little League."

Ms. Honeycott's only comment was her nice tinkly laugh. And Anthony was soon out the door, wishing he could have somehow found the words to express his unhappiness. Yet what good were words? They never changed anything.

That same afternoon Mr. Diamond once again accompanied Anthony to baseball practice. If Anthony's fielding left something to be desired, it was always worse with Mr. Diamond watching. Today was no exception. Even Anthony's batting was off.

Usually the coach did his utmost to avoid Mr. Diamond. Today, after the session, he sought him out. Although they stood talking a good distance from him, Anthony could hear a little of the conversation, something about the plywood board he'd told the coach he was using for practice. Anthony caught a few of the man's words. ". . . not a good idea . . . slows him down." Something about precision coming later.

No one had any trouble hearing Mr. Diamond. "Now look, fella. You trying to tell *me* about baseball? I was playing baseball before you were knee high to a grasshopper. Why, I forgot more than you'll ever know. You guys call yourselves coaches. From what I see, you don't know any more than your average spectator. Your average spectator don't know from beans, but that don't stop him from sounding like an authority."

The coach's face reddened, but he talked in subdued tones. Anthony heard him say, "Well, it's up to you."

"You're darn tootin' it's up to me," Mr. Diamond said and stalked off.

The only good thing about the set-to was that all the way home Mr. Diamond was so busy laying out the coach he forgot to lay out Anthony for his poor day's showing.

Anthony sat in the dugout still astonished to realize that, in the Padres' first official game of the season, he was not only in the opening lineup as first baseman but fourth in the batting order. He'd heard one of the boys say that fourth position at bat was the clean-up batter. Everyone expected you to drive in any of the first three ahead of you. Anthony wasn't quite sure he liked that responsibility.

Still, some of his team's excitement had started to rub off on him. First, there was his new uniform, a little baggy, perhaps, yet it made him feel like someone else. Tony Lang, first baseman? The League board had scheduled Anthony's team to play the Astros on their home field. As visiting team, the Padres had warmed up first. Anthony could tell they were all about as nervous as he was. Small wonder. In practice games, there was never this kind of noise and activity, people scrambling over each other to take places in the stands, little kids screaming their heads off, the loudspeaker blasting out names, field positions, and the batting order. It gave you the feeling something important was going on.

And all too soon, it seemed, the Astros were out on the field, the Padres' first batter in the batter's box, and the umpire calling "Play." The game had begun.

Chuck Finney was first at bat. It surprised Anthony to realize he knew all of the kids' names now and a good deal about their games. Chuck was a good fielder but a weak hitter.

Someone yelled from the stands, "Come on, Smiley, give it to him!"

You didn't have to guess who Smiley was. The Astros' pitcher looked as if he'd been born smiling. Anthony kept his eye on him to see if he could figure out his technique. He watched Smiley wind up, then let go with a fast ball. Chuck, overly eager, swung too soon. "Strike one," the umpire called. Another of Smiley's fast balls came at Chuck. Strike two. Smiley's next pitch was a change of pace. Chuck, obviously expecting a fast ball, again swung at the wrong moment. Strike three. Out.

Anthony groaned. What a beginning. Up to this

point, he'd always felt a little indifferent about their games. With that quick Out, he suddenly began to grow more involved.

With the next batter, Smiley's pitching went a little sour. After one strike, the hitter worked the count to three-and-two, fouled off the next pitch, then drew a walk. Smiley walked the next batter, too. Still smiling though.

Then it was Anthony's turn. He came up to the batter's box, feeling somewhat reassured. At least he wasn't about to face any hot-shot pitcher. He took position and swung the bat to get the feel of it. Then Smiley began winding up, that big grin still plastered all over his face. It was almost unnerving. How could a guy smile through everything and anything? Anthony might have been staring at the Cheshire cat. Everything seemed to fade away except that big grin. When Smiley let go the ball, Anthony tore his eyes away a second too late, then swung. Strike one.

He could have kicked himself. He had known the pitch would be a fast ball, and it was. Smiley's pattern was fast ball, fast ball, change of pace. Anthony had let that smile hypnotize him. Cool it, he told himself. Keep your eye on the ball.

Smiley's next pitch was again a fast ball. But not fast enough. This time Anthony was ready. He drove sharply to left field, then ran like mad to first. When he heard all the yelling from the stands, he realized his hit had brought home one of the Padres and advanced the other to third. Things were looking up. Right after that, Smiley walked the next two batters, giving the Padres still another run. Now we're getting someplace, Anthony thought from third base. Unfortunately, the next two batters struck out for the second and third outs. Now the Padres took the field and the Astros were coming to bat.

The Padres' two-run lead held through the first five Astros batters. With two out and the bases loaded, the sixth batter grounded the ball to the third baseman who bobbled it. Before he could recover, the runner on third scored and everyone moved around one base. Then, to Anthony's relief, the next batter struck out. The inning ended with the Padres' lead at two to one.

In the second inning, Anthony came up to bat with two out and runners on first and second. Smiley had walked both of them. He seemed a little mad about that. He wasn't exactly smiling now. Baring his teeth was more like it. His first pitch went wild. Anthony backed away and took it. "Ball one," the umpire called.

Smiley wound up again. This time the ball came right toward the plate. Anthony swung with everything he had. *Whack!* It sounded as if he'd cracked the bat. Without even waiting to see where the ball was heading, he took to his heels, running for all he was worth for first, then on to second. Rounding second, he could see that the runner ahead of him was clapping his hands and just jogging around third. Beyond third, he saw the whole Padre team suddenly explode off the bench. "It's a homer! A homer! A THREE-RUN HOMER!"

The cheering from the stands drowned out any boos coming from the other side. All the Padres were yelling like crazy and pounding Anthony on the back. "Nice going, Tony," Anthony heard all around him. He was embarrassed and pleased at the same time. His batting had made four runs for his team, Smiley's pitching another. Anthony couldn't get over what he'd done. He went through the rest of the inning feeling slightly dazed. When the second ended, he had to look up at the scoreboard to make sure he wasn't dreaming. No, there it was in big numbers, 5–1.

"Good work, Tony," the coach said, then to Anthony's surprise, told him to make it to the bench. Four of the others in the opening lineup joined him as new players took their places. Anthony felt a little disappointed. What had he done wrong? Even in the field he hadn't pulled any real boners.

As he watched the third inning, he began to feel grateful that he *was* sitting on the bench. The kid who had relieved Smiley was a much better pitcher, really first-rate. Anthony had the feeling he never would have made that homer with this new boy on the mound. He found himself so thoroughly caught up in the rest of the game he might have been playing it. He yelled just as loud as the other Padres, experiencing a new feeling of camaraderie with them.

All through the fourth he sat restlessly watching the Astros chalk up four runs. In the fifth, when they made a homer that tied the score, Anthony itched to get at a bat. And in the sixth, when they made yet another run, he booed with the rest of his team and called it beginner's luck. The game ended with the Astros winning six to five. Losing was a great disappointment, but in going over each play with the other Padres, Anthony had to agree it could have gone a lot worse for them.

As everything started to break up, he suddenly realized that, all the while, he had never given a thought to the Diamonds. Now he saw Mr. Diamond striding across the field, making straight for the coach. There was something about that purposeful gait that made Anthony tense.

The coach was about to head toward the parking lot when Mr. Diamond called, "Now just a darned minute there. I got something I want to say to you."

The coach turned around, frowning. "Yes?"

"You just tell me what you think you're doing."

"What do you mean?"

"I want to know why a kid who can chalk up home runs only gets to play two innings."

The coach's glance took in all the eyes turned on them. "This is no place to talk."

"As good a place as any. I intend to have this out right here and now."

"Now, look, I had my reasons for using Tony in only the first two innings."

"Sure you did. All the kids have to play a minimum of two innings. But you can bet I know what your real reasons are. You didn't like what I told you a while back. Hit too close to home, didn't I? Now you're trying to take it out on my kid. Well, nobody gets away with that with Ed Diamond. No, sir."

It was obvious that the coach was growing angrier by the second and trying to control it. "I'm not here to fight with parents. I'm here to train boys to play baseball. And I'll do it in my own way. I put Tony in the first two innings because I knew he'd be facing a weak pitcher. I knew he'd have a chance to score. In my judgment, he needs to gain confidence right now. I don't think he's quite ready for a more experienced pitcher. And I just happen to think it more important to build confidence in a boy than tear it down."

Mr. Diamond sneered. "Listen, fella, I wasn't born yesterday. You're not talking to one of your eleven-year-olds. Nobody pulls the wool over Ed Diamond's eyes. You got it in for me. You even sacrificed the game because of it. Don't think I don't know what's going on—and I'm not standing still for it."

"If you have a complaint, you know where you can take it."

"Oh, you'd like that, wouldn't you? And I know how far that would get me. All you guys stick together—cut from the same cloth, all of you. Bunch of two-bit bench-sitters—never made it yourselves in baseball. Makes you feel important to push a bunch of kids around. Well, not my kid, you don't. You know why? Because I'm taking him out right now. You don't get my kid to kick around any more." The owl eyes searched the field until they spotted Anthony. "Come on, Tony. Let's get out of this two-ring circus."

Anthony, feeling stunned, trailed Mr. Diamond out the gate, aware all eyes were following the two of them. Mr. Diamond turned back to him and said, "You take off that outfit when you get home, and I'll turn it in."

Anthony's eyes swept over his baggy uniform. It was all over. Just like that. *All over.* He couldn't believe it.

⑥

Pretty Danged Good

After school Anthony worked at the Goodwill desk, P–51 parts strewn all over the top. With all the recent Little League activity, he'd had no time to give to his model. Now he had too much.

In the week that had passed since the game, the wire fence in the backyard had come down, and the plywood board had found a place among scrap wood in the garage. If anyone dared mention Little League around Mr. Diamond, he ran the risk of having his head snapped off. In fact, no matter what the topic of conversation, Mr. Diamond was snapping off heads aplenty that week.

Finally, sounding as if he was trying to convince himself, he said to Anthony, "It's probably all for the best. You know, Tony, to get any place in baseball, you got to be an all-around player. Your fielding wasn't any good. Probably wouldn't have got much better neither. You're either cut out for the game or you're not." Instead of looking at Anthony as he talked, his eyes seemed to consult some higher authority. The Lord? "Yup, all for the best. Can't make a silk purse out of a sow's ear."

After that, Hildy came in for a lot of his Shut ups. Anthony, he ignored in a strange, hostile way that made the boy feel that everything that had happened was his fault. If he'd only been a silk purse Mr. Diamond would still be a baseball hero.

Now, as Anthony absently fitted one plastic part to the other, he felt all closed within himself. Numb. He looked up to see Mrs. Diamond at the door of his room.

"Working on your airplane?" she asked.

Anyone could see that he was. "Uh huh." He picked up a wing and, although it didn't need it, began to furiously rub sandpaper over it, hoping she would leave.

Instead she came in and stared down at his work. "I just bet you'll have a real nice plane when you get through." Anthony said nothing. She stood there uneasily for a moment. Finally she said, "I hope you don't feel too bad about Little League, Tony."

He sanded even harder. "Naw—didn't want to play baseball anyhow."

When he offered nothing further, she gave a troubled nod and started to leave. Before she reached the door, Anthony looked up and, with an anger that almost bordered on tears, said, "Why'd he make me play anyhow?"

She came back into the room and sat down in a chair

near the desk. "You know what I think? I think he feels real bad about all this—maybe even worse than you. He always gets mad too fast. Then he does things without thinking—you know, kind of like cutting off your nose to spite your face. I guess sometimes we hurt ourselves more than anybody else."

Anthony stared down glumly at his model. "Well, I don't see why he wanted me to play in the first place."

Mrs. Diamond sighed. "I'm not much at figuring out what's inside folks, but sometimes I think no matter how grown up we get, there's still a child in all of us. Some folks more than others. You know what I mean?"

Anthony shook his head.

"I mean, even after we're big, we can still act like kids. And sometimes that's good, and sometimes it's bad. Dad never had any real childhood. Maybe it's worse for people like that."

Dad? Anthony still couldn't bring himself to call the man Dad. Yet Mr. Diamond had called Anthony his kid. But he's not my dad, Anthony thought, and I'm not his kid. He said, "Everybody has a childhood."

"No, Tony," she said, her voice gentle, "everybody is at some time a child, but not everybody has a childhood. Dad was an orphan. His aunt and uncle raised him along with all their kids. They lived on a farm in Missouri and all the kids had to work hard from the time they were little. As soon as he could, Dad got a job, quit school and got away from the place."

"Well, he must have played baseball when he was

little." Mr. Diamond always acted as if, all his life, he'd done nothing else.

"Maybe a little. But I don't think there was time for much of anything you could call play."

So the man was a liar, too. Or was he only one of those spectators who didn't know from beans but that didn't stop him from sounding like an authority?

Mrs. Diamond said, "I guess maybe that's why Dad wanted a son so much. Sometimes when you've done without something, you want your kids to have it. Or you want them to do the things you never had a chance to do. I don't mean it's right. Most times, all it means is you want a second chance at being a child yourself. Like, if you never got to play baseball but your boy does, then you get a little of the fun, too, and you don't feel so cheated."

"Then why didn't he put Hildy in Little League? She plays baseball in school. One of the kids said they were taking girls now."

Mrs. Diamond smiled a little sadly. "Dad's kind of old fashioned about girls. He doesn't hold with women wanting to be truck drivers or playing baseball." She gave a deep sigh. "I just guess it was a real sad day for him when Hildy was born. For her, too, sometimes. She can't help being a girl, and he can't help wanting a boy."

Trying to be helpful, Anthony said, "Maybe you could have more children. Most likely some of them would be boys."

She laughed, then got up and roughed his hair. "No, Tony. Hildy's our first and last." Then she started from the room, pausing at the door to add, "Unless you ever decide you want to be one of the family."

Anthony stared after her, feeling outraged, Decide to become one of the weirdo Diamonds? Never. Never, never, never!

A little later that same afternoon Anthony heard the doorbell. At the third persistent ring, he realized no one was answering, so he ran downstairs and opened the door. The man on the other side stood there staring at him for a moment. Anthony stared, too. The man's short, wiry haircut made him look as if his hair was standing on end. And his dark, double-breasted suit, a little tight, seemed like the kind of thing men wore at funerals, except that the collar of a bright yellow sports shirt sat outside this one.

"Y'all live here?" the man asked, looking puzzled.

"Yes."

"Shoot! You mean I got the wrong house?" He peered around to glance at the street number on the stucco beside the door. "The Diamonds don't live here?"

"Oh, yes, they live here."

The man looked even more puzzled. "I always thought Margie and Ed had a girl."

"They do—Hildy. I just live with them."

"Humph." The man obviously had more important

things on his mind than Anthony's status in the family.
He brusquely pushed past and into the hall. Before
Anthony closed the door, he noticed a new Ford sitting
at the curb. When he turned around, the man was giving the hall a good looking over. "Where's Margie?" he
asked.

"I guess she's around someplace."

"Well, you just go get her for me, huh?" He made
the demand sound like a question. Then he started pacing the hall.

Anthony found Mrs. Diamond coming in from the
backyard. "A man wants to see me?" she said, looking
surprised. She took a moment to remove the apron she
wore and smooth her dress before following Anthony
out to the hall. When she saw the visitor, she stopped
and regarded him quizzically. "Edgar Doyle. . . ?" He
stopped his pacing and spun around to face her. "Oh,
my goodness, it is you." She looked all flustered.

He went over to her, put his arms around her and
gave her a big hug. When he released her, he said,
"Well, looks to me like you and Ed are doing right good
for yourselves." He gestured around the hall. "I reckon,
in California, a big house like this set you back a pile of
bucks."

Mrs. Diamond had to explain that they'd bought the
place long before prices had sky-rocketed. And, of
course, it had needed so many repairs they'd paid less.
When she finished making what sounded like an apol-
ogy, she said, "Well, I just guess you're about the last

person I expected to see when I walked out in the hall. Almost didn't recognize you."

He patted his belly. "Well, I put on a couple of pounds—all that good livin'." He chuckled. "Where's Ed?"

"At work. He'll be home about six."

His nod accepted and dismissed the information. "Bessie Mae and me got us a new house, too, last year—had it built—great big place, bigger than this, I reckon. Well, the kids needed more room. And you know how it is, man in business like me has to put up a front."

"That's nice, Edgar Doyle. Guess you must be doing real good."

"Can't complain."

She stood there for a moment, looking at a loss. Then she put an arm around Anthony and said, "This here's Tony Lang. He's come to live with us for a while." When her brother looked right through Anthony and failed to comment, she said, "Well, come on in and sit down. I'll go fix a room for you."

He put up a hand to stop her. "Can't stay but a minute. Flew out here on business for Bessie Mae's daddy. Figure I'll find me a room in Hollywood tonight, see the sights, then get over to Los Angeles first thing in the morning. I'll take care of the business and be on my way back to New Mexico by afternoon. Had to rent me a car, so I figured, while I was so close, I'd better look in on you folks."

"How are Bessie Mac and the kids?"

A look of grave concern came over his face. "Well now, that's what I come to see you about. As long as I been married to Bessie Mae, I never seen her so upset before. I tell you, Margie, you got to put a stop to them letters Ma's been sending."

At the mention of letters, Anthony, who had been trying to ease away, perked up his ears instead.

"Letters?" Mrs. Diamond looked puzzled. Then she glanced back toward her mother's room. "Maybe we'd better go in the front room and talk." She opened the door off the hall and said to Anthony, "Would you light the furnace, Tony? That room's kind of chilly this time of year."

Anthony followed them into the living room and, although it was a simple job, took his time about lighting the floor furnace. Now he was beginning to wonder if he'd done something wrong in mailing the old woman's letters.

As they were seating themselves, Mrs. Diamond said, "I don't know nothing about any letters, Edgar Doyle."

A glint of suspicion showed in his eyes. "Margie, you told us on the phone—must have been two years ago now—you said Ma don't even go out of the house. Must have been somebody mailing them letters."

"I just don't know—unless Hildy—but we gave her strict orders not to."

Anthony pretended to be very busy with the furnace. Neither one of them paid him any attention.

Edgar Doyle said, "I tell you, Margie, you got to put a stop to it. Ma sounds like you folks got her locked in a cell or something. Keeps writing about how I got to come and get her, how we'll get a little house near the ranch—well, *you* know I ain't worked on the Stubbins' ranch for well on to twenty years now."

"Ma's a little senile, Edgar Doyle. She forgets."

He ignored her. "Then she either sounds like Bessie Mae is dead, or she makes real poisonous remarks about her—about how she's glad I never took up with that girl who lived out on the flats, how you can't trust any girl that dyes her hair. Well, *you* know Bessie Mae ain't never dyed her hair."

Mrs. Diamond was noticeably quiet.

"I tell you, Margie, I got a good thing going with Bessie Mae's daddy. He took me into his plumbing business, taught me everything I know. In a couple of years, he's going to retire and turn the whole kit and caboodle over to me. Don't know what he'd think if he saw them crazy letters. Might think craziness runs in the family."

"Ma's not crazy! Don't you ever say that, Edgar Doyle."

"Well, you know what I mean." He sounded sullen.

There was a long silence. Finally, in a weary voice, Mrs. Diamond said, "We've had Ma for a long time now—almost ten years. All I ever hear is how bad I treat her and how good you always were to her. Maybe it's time you did your share, Edgar Doyle. Even if you just took her for a—"

"You know I can't do that! Bessie Mae couldn't take care of no crazy old lady. Bessie Mae's not strong like you. She's delicate."

Another long silence. Then, "Does she still weigh a hundred and eighty pounds?"

"Now don't you go making no poisonous remarks, Margie. Just because a woman's got a little fat on her don't mean she can't be as delicate as a skinny woman—maybe more. Why, Bessie Mae ails all the time." He paused, righteous indignation stamped all over his face. "Besides, we may have to take in her daddy one of these days. He's no youngster—never can tell about those things."

Anthony knew he was tinkering too long when Mrs. Diamond said, "Don't you know how to work it, Tony?"

"I think I got it now," he said, sounding as if he'd been busily trying to figure it out. The furnace came on with a small explosion.

Mrs. Diamond stood up. "Tony, you keep my brother company while I get Ma ready to see him." She turned back to Edgar Doyle. "Long as you're here, you'd better see Ma."

"Oh— Well, all right." He sounded none too enthusiastic.

After she'd left, he asked Anthony why he was living there. When Anthony told him, his only comment was, "Humph," after which he fell silent. It seemed forever before Mrs. Diamond returned with her mother.

As the old woman shuffled into the room, Anthony noticed she had on a fancier robe than the flannel she usually wore, and her teeth were in place. She looked around, a bewildered expression on her face.

"I'll make some coffee," Mrs. Diamond said and disappeared.

Edgar Doyle got up, strode across the room, put his arms around his mother, said "Hi, Sweetheart. How's my best girl?" and gave her a walloping hug and a sloppy kiss.

As if trying to clear away a haze, she blinked her eyes and stared up at him. "Is it really you, boy?"

"Don't you know me, Ma?"

"Edgar Doyle—it *is* you. 'Course I know my own boy. First, I thought Margie was funning me." She dropped her cane and flung her arms around him. Tears began to stream down her face. "I know'd you'd come, boy, know'd you'd take me away."

He patted her back, then eased her from him and made her sit on the couch. "Now, Ma, you got a real nice place here. Bessie Mae and me only got us a li'l biddy old house—hardly room for the kids."

"Bessie Mae?" she said vaguely.

"You got to remember Bessie Mae, Ma. You were there when we got married."

She shook her head as if to clear it. "I forget sometimes."

He sat down and put an arm around her. "Now I can't see my best girl in no li'l biddy old house with a bunch of noisy kids and not even a room to call her own. Why, I don't even know where we'd put you. Guess we'd just have to stick you out in the garage, danged if we wouldn't." He laughed as if he'd made a good joke.

"The garage," she repeated, her eyes foggy.

"Now, you wouldn't want to live in no garage, would you, Sweetheart?"

The old woman dully moved her head from side to side.

"No, not my girl. Not when she can live in a big house like this with a room all to herself and her own television set—oh, yes, I've heard all about you from Margie." He chucked her under the chin. "Now, I'd say that was having things pretty danged good. What would you say?"

"Eh?" The old woman cupped her ear with a hand as if his voice were coming to her from far away, perhaps from out of the past.

"I said, 'I'd say pretty danged good. What would you say?' "

A soft chuckle began to issue from her throat. "I'd say, pretty danged good."

"There, you see, you *do* remember things. You remembered our old game."

Perhaps she had forgotten what she wanted of her son, for her face brightened now. "You always was a big kidder."

Somehow Anthony didn't feel that he wanted to hear

more. He got up and slipped out the door as she said, "Remember how you used to bring me chocolates, Edgar Doyle? 'For my best girl,' you'd always say."

Anthony paused outside, listening to the hollow sound of laughter echo through the room. For the first time, he felt a warm rush of pity for the old woman. After a moment, he decided he'd better find Mrs. Diamond and tell her he had mailed all those letters, but he wouldn't do it any more. After that, maybe he should raid his money box, walk over to the shopping center and buy Mrs. Puckett a pound of chocolates.

7

A Real Thoroughbred Siamese

"Mrs. Diamond's been telling me a lot of nice things about you, Anthony," Ms. Honeycott said. "She says you've been helping her wait on her mother."

Anthony looked down at his shoes. "I just take in trays and stuff like that. It isn't anything."

"I think it's very considerate."

Anthony knew better. It had more to do with his guilt about the chocolates he'd never bought for the old woman. He'd really meant to. Yet when he opened the Chinese puzzle box and counted twenty-two dollars and seventy-six cents, his generous impulse fled. That was all the money he had in the world. What if he wanted to run away? He'd need every cent. Or what if his father should come for him and not have a job? They could eat for a long time on that much money.

Ms. Honeycott said, "I imagine Mrs. Puckett appreciates your help, too."

"I dunno." Strange about the old woman. She

seemed to have forgotten that her son had ever visited her. She was still as irritable as ever, yelling for Margie every fifteen minutes. When Anthony appeared instead, she seemed rattled, not quite sure about how to take him. But, at least, she wasn't handing him letters to mail now.

"Anything you want to tell me, Anthony?"

He glanced up to find Ms. Honeycott's eyes more true-blue than ever. And fixed on him. "No."

"What about Little League?"

"Aw—I didn't want to play baseball anyhow."

"Well, maybe you don't have to tell me. I think I can pretty much put the story together from what Mrs. Diamond said." She regarded him thoughtfully. "Anthony, how would you like to live someplace else?"

"Where?"

"With a different family."

He shrugged. What good was living with a different family? They'd probably be as bad as the Diamonds. Or worse. "I might as well stay where I am. My dad will most likely be settled any day now. I wouldn't get to stay anyplace very long."

"Anthony, what do I keep telling you?"

He reached for a glass paperweight on her desk, held it up to catch the light, and pretended to be wrapped up in its design. That was better than going through all that reality business again.

She sighed. "We still haven't heard from your dad. Until we do, I'd like to feel that you were well placed."

"I'm okay."

She stared at him again, looking troubled. Finally she said, "Well, for now, we'll wait and see how things go. All right?"

"Oh, sure," he said.

It was a dull Saturday afternoon. Anthony worked on his model, but he felt listless. Mrs. Diamond was out shopping, Mr. Diamond at church, helping volunteers paint the annex. Or, more likely, bossing the job. Hildy was off visiting somebody in the neighborhood. Except for the sound of Mrs. Puckett's television set, the house was quiet. To fill time, Anthony decided to take his model outdoors and try some silver spray paint on it.

As he was setting up in the backyard, Hildy came through the gate, a young Siamese cat in her arms. Curious, Anthony opened his mouth to ask her about the animal, then remembered he wasn't really on speaking terms with Hildy. Instead, he pretended he was too busy to notice her. But all the while, he secretly watched. He saw her glance around with a kind of lost look. Her eyes rested on him speculatively for a moment. Finally she placed the cat on the grass, then flopped down beside and began to play with the animal.

It was hardly more than a kitten, Anthony saw. Somehow he felt that big lump inside him again. In the old days, when his mother was alive, there had always been a cat or a kitten running around their house. In the old days. . . . Now, as this one scampered about

Hildy, he found it difficult to keep up his pose of indifference. She had turned over on her stomach, he noticed. The cat licked her nose and she giggled. Which surprised Anthony. He had no idea that anything could tickle Hildy.

As he went about arranging scrap lumber into a crude paint booth, the cat deserted her to investigate the fascinating project. Cautiously, it sniffed wood, sniffed Anthony's sneakers, apparently decided that neither were enemies, then promptly got a claw-hold on Anthony's jeans and, through cloth and flesh, began to scramble up his leg.

"Ouch, that hurts!" Anthony pulled the cat free. He knew Hildy's eyes were on him. Without so much as a pat, he placed the kitten on the ground. Immediately the animal tore up Anthony's leg again. "Ow!"

This time Hildy began to laugh.

"It's not funny. That hurts," he said as he extricated himself from the needle-sharp claws. This time he picked up the animal. When he looked down to find two very blue and very crossed eyes staring up at him, in spite of himself, he had to smile. "He's cross-eyed," he said.

"He's lost," Hildy said.

So that was what all this was about. "How do you know?"

"Because he was here when I went out and when I came back. And he wouldn't go away. And he looked lost. So I took him up and down the street, then as far as two streets over and nobody knows who he belongs to."

"He's got to belong to somebody."

"I know. He's a real thoroughbred Siamese."

"Yeah," Anthony said without thinking, then took a closer look at the cat. "How do you know he's a thoroughbred?"

"Because he wouldn't look like a Siamese if he wasn't. The Siamese traits are recessive. Our teacher told us."

Anthony had no idea what recessive meant, but he wasn't about to admit it.

Hildy said. "If you breed an alley cat with a Siamese, you don't get any kittens that look Siamese. They're all alley cats."

"Oh."

"Besides, he's cross-eyed. That's from inbreeding."

It occurred to Anthony that this was the longest conversation Hildy had ever held with him. It also occurred to him that she wanted something. Help? Advice? The cat nuzzled his ear. "What are you going to do about him?"

Hildy, looking perplexed, got to her feet. "I don't know."

To Anthony, her indecision seemed silly. There were perfectly reasonable ways to deal with the stray animal problem. You simply put a "Found" ad in the papers, and if no one answered, you kept the animal yourself. "Well, the first thing you'd better do is feed him. If he's lost, he's probably hungry." He walked over and handed the cat to her.

Hildy cuddled it, then glanced toward the house. "Anybody home yet?"

"Only your grandmother."

"I guess I'll take him in and give him some milk."

Anthony followed her into the kitchen where Hildy poured milk into a saucer. In short order, the cat lapped it up and, in a raucous voice, demanded more. "He really *is* hungry," Hildy said and filled the saucer again. Then she investigated the refrigerator. "There's some leftover pot roast. Do you think he'd eat something like that?"

"Sure."

She took out a big hunk of meat and moved to give it to the cat.

Anthony's voice stopped her. "A cat can't eat anything that big! You've got to cut it up in little pieces."

"How do *you* know?"

"Because that's what we always did for our cats." He took the meat from her hand, found a knife in a drawer and began cutting. Hildy might know a lot about recessives, but she sure didn't know much about cats.

"I never had a cat," she said as if answering his thoughts.

"I've had tons of them." He couldn't help exaggerating, because, for once, he felt superior.

The cat finished the milk, greedily gobbled up the

meat, burped, then with eyes that asked for more, stared up at them.

"I can't figure out if he's looking at me or at you," Anthony said.

Hildy giggled. "He looks so funny with those eyes."

"Yeah, kind of sincere."

"Sincere?" She cocked her head and studied the animal. "He really *does*. Maybe that's what I'll call him—Sincere."

"Hey, that's great. If anybody wants to know his name, you can say, 'My cat is Sincere.' "

When Hildy began to laugh, Anthony felt as if he'd made the best joke of the year. He started to laugh, too.

Only Sincere seemed unimpressed with Anthony's wit. He ignored the frivolity for the more serious business of a thorough wash-up. When they again behaved sensibly, sitting on the floor at his level, giving him the attention he deserved, he abandoned his toilet to lavish rough-tongued approval on each of them.

It was hard for Anthony to imagine that this Hildy was the same girl who had always acted so nasty. Now, with her interest in the kitten, her former animosity seemed forgotten.

Sincere had a full repertoire of kitten tricks which he performed most willingly. First, there was The Great Cheek-nuzzling Trick, then The Famous Collar Trick in which he wrapped himself around Hildy's neck and hung limp like a fur piece. After that, came The Flying

Leap from her shoulder to Anthony's. He even treated them to a few of his lesser accomplishments, like Tail-chasing and, when provided with small objects that he could easily bat around, Stalking the Wild Beast.

They were both so caught up in his antics they were unaware of anything else until a voice at the door said, "What's going on here?" and Mr. Diamond, in paint-spattered clothes, strode into the room.

Hildy snatched up the kitten and held it protectively against her.

Mr. Diamond's thick-spectacled eyes instantly took in the situation. A flush of rage spread over his face. In a menacing tone, he said, "Hildy, what did I tell you the last time?"

"He was lost. I didn't—"

"I told you if you ever brought another animal into this house, you wouldn't be able to sit down for a week. Now you get that thing out of here. Right now. Then I'll give you something you won't forget."

Anthony had the feeling her father would have wal-loped Hildy right there and then except for the cat in her arms. Instead he kept a good distance from the two of them. Hildy opened her mouth to speak. As usual she was going to put up an argument, Anthony guessed. Quickly, he said, "It wasn't Hildy's fault—it was mine." He wasn't quite sure what prompted his gallantry, but, at least, it kept her from provoking her father even more.

Mr. Diamond's eyes traveled from her to Anthony. "Huh?" The word came out like a grunt.

"I did it. I brought the cat in."

"You brought the cat in?" He sounded as if he needed a moment to cope with this new development.

"I didn't know I shouldn't." Anthony talked fast. "He was lost and he's a real thoroughbred Siamese. He must be worth a lot of money. I thought I'd better try to find his owner."

For a moment Mr. Diamond seemed at a loss for words. Then he said gruffly, "Yeah—well— Don't ever do a thing like that again. I'll be sneezing and coughing for weeks from that thing. Get it out of here. Put it in the garage, and I'll call the pound. They can find the owner."

"No!" Hildy cried. "I won't let you send him to the pound. They kill animals. I read it in the paper." She clutched Sincere tighter.

Oh, no, Anthony thought. If she'd only learn to keep her mouth shut. Before her father could open his, Anthony said, "He probably lives someplace in the neighborhood. I'll take him around and see if I can find his owner."

Mr. Diamond glanced from Hildy to Anthony, a frustrated look on his face. All that anger and no place to direct it. "I don't care what you do. Just get that thing out of here." He turned on his heel and marched out of the kitchen.

"Come on," Anthony said to Hildy and they both scooted out the back door.

Outside, Hildy said, "Why'd you do that?"

"Do what?"

"Take the blame."

Anthony thought about it now. "I don't know—seemed like the easiest way. Besides, it *was* my fault. I suggested it. And after all, he couldn't do anything to me. Nobody told *me* cats made him sneeze, and I shouldn't bring them into the house."

"He has an allergy. I guess, even if you brought one in, he wouldn't hit you anyhow."

"Why not?"

"Because you're a foster."

"A foster?" She made it sound like a last name. "Yeah, I guess I am," he said thoughtfully. If people only clobbered their own kids, maybe there was some advantage in being a foster, after all. Anthony fastened his eyes on the cat instead of on Hildy as he said, "I don't want to tell you what to do," then immediately set about telling her what to do, "but you shouldn't keep answering him back and arguing with him when he gets mad. If you'd just keep quiet, he wouldn't do anything to you."

"Well, I can't help it." Her voice was sullen. "It's the way I'm made or something." She stroked Sincere's head and changed the subject. "What are we going to do about him? I've already been all over trying to find out who he belongs to."

"I know. Well, there's only one other thing we *can* do."

"What?"

"Try to find a good home for him. That's better than sending him to the pound."

"Suppose no one will take him?"

"They'll take him," he assured her. "And we'll be fussy about who gets him, too. After all, he's a real thoroughbred Siamese."

8

The Third Degree

"And you said we wouldn't have any trouble." Hildy, her arms full of Sincere, blew a stray wisp of hair from her forehead.

"I can't figure it out," Anthony said. "You'd think everybody would want a Siamese."

They had thoroughly canvassed four blocks. Some people already had cats. Some disliked them. Others had dogs. Big vicious dogs that bared their fangs and terrified Sincere. Little yappy dogs that made him spit in disdain. One woman opened her door to them, spotted the kitten, threw up her arms, let out a blood-curdling scream, then slammed the door in their faces.

As they trudged on, Hildy said, "If you ask me, she's an ailurophobe."

"Well, she sure wasn't very nice. I could think up a few dirty names to call her myself."

Hildy began to laugh. "That's not a dirty name. It means she's got cat phobia. She's scared of them."

80

It took a moment for Anthony to absorb the information, then he acted as if he'd known it all along. "I was just making a joke," he said in a tone that pitied anyone who couldn't understand that.

"Oh— Oh, I get it." She began to giggle.

Hildy sure knew a lot of big words, Anthony thought. You had to admire someone who knew a lot of big words. You also had to watch yourself. "You getting tired? You want me to hold him for a while?"

"No, I like holding him." She shifted the cat, and he snuggled against her. "I sure hope we find a home for him."

"Yeah. I guess we'll just have to stop being so fussy about who gets him," he said, really trying to make a joke this time.

"Fussy? No one's even given us the chance," she said, dead serious, then caught herself. "Oh, I get it." She began to giggle again. "You know, you've got a pretty good sense of humor."

Anthony gave her his it's-really-nothing shrug. They walked up and down another block, ringing doorbells, but there were still no takers for Sincere. Anthony said, "We'd have better luck selling candy for Boy Scouts."

Instead of a giggle now, Hildy gave a tired smile. "It sure seems hopeless. What are we going to do?"

"Keep trying. There isn't anything else we *can* do. We've got to find a home for him tonight."

They turned down a side street and tried two more houses without success. At the third house, they walked up the stairs to the porch in dejected silence. Anthony rang the bell. In a few moments a boy, all ears and red hair, answered the door. Anthony opened his mouth to start his spiel, then took a second look at the boy. "Hey, I know you. You're in my room at school."

The boy stared at Anthony for a moment before recognition flashed in his eyes. "Oh, sure—you sit next to Rocky Schuller. You're Lang."

"Tony. You're Smithson."

"Smitty."

Hildy cleared her throat, and Anthony remembered why they were there. He pointed to Sincere. "We're trying to find a home for our thoroughbred Siamese cat." Three streets back they had discovered the truth was only defeating their purpose. Everyone was more interested in giving advice on finding the cat's owner than in taking the cat. So Hildy and Anthony had decided to alter the facts slightly. Although it cut down considerably on conversation, it had brought no better results.

Or had it? Anthony saw a big grin spread over Smitty's face. "Wow, a Siamese," he said.

Anthony's and Hildy's eyes met. Hopeful?

"I always wanted a Siamese." Smitty reached over and scratched the kitten's head. "We had to put our cat, Toughy, to sleep a few months ago."

Anthony looked at Hildy. Hildy looked at Anthony. Eureka! Rush him now. Don't give him a chance to think it over. Zero right in, get his name on the dotted line, and close the deal.

Anthony took Sincere from Hildy's arms and placed him in Smitty's. "Feel how soft he is."

Smitty stroked the kitten. "He's a little guy."

"Five months old," Hildy said.

Anthony's expression asked her how she knew. She gave an imperceptible shrug and head shake. She didn't.

Sincere jockeyed himself up to Smitty's shoulder, came a cropper with a big car, took a second to decide what to do about it, then figured out a sensible solution. When in doubt, wash.

"Hey, that tickles." Smitty began to laugh as Sincere, very business-like, ran his tongue into an area too often forgotten by the washcloth.

As Smitty, still laughing, tried to interest the kitten in less ticklish parts of his anatomy, Anthony winked at Hildy. With thumb and index finger, he gave her a quick O sign. Deal sewed up.

Then Smitty said, "I'll have to ask my mom."

Deal unsewed. Drag a second party into a transaction and complications are sure to arise.

"Come on in," Smitty said. "My mom's out in the kitchen. We'll go back and ask her."

When they walked into the room, Smitty's mother was busy beating something in a bowl. A cake-mix box sat on the counter. A little girl of about seven, red-headed like Smitty, was overseeing the operation. Unlike her children, Mrs. Smithson had black hair. Probably something to do with recessives, Anthony thought.

The little girl spotted the kitten in Smitty's arms.

"Ooooh, a Siamese. Where'd you get him?" She ran over and began to pat Sincere's head.

Smitty's mother stopped her beating and turned around. "Well, what have we here?"

Smitty pointed to Anthony and Hildy. "They're trying to find a home for their cat. Can we take him, Mom?"

Smitty's sister started hopping up and down. "Oh, please, Mom, can we?"

Mrs. Smithson, a plump, good-natured looking woman, said, "Why do you want to give away such a pretty cat?"

Hildy shook her head sadly. "We can't keep him. My dad has an allergy."

"Oh, that's too bad."

"He's a thoroughbred Siamese. We're trying to find him a good home," Anthony said.

"Does he have papers?"

Anthony glanced quickly to Hildy. "Well—no."

"But that doesn't mean he's not a thoroughbred." For Mrs. Smithson's benefit, Hildy went all through her recessives again.

"I see." The woman looked amused. "Is he neutered?"

There was a long pause as Anthony's and Hildy's eyes met and locked. Yes? No?

Smitty apparently thought they didn't understand. "She means, is he fixed?"

Hildy finally said, "You're not supposed to fix them until they're eight months old."

Was she guessing again? Even if she was, you had to say this for the girl, she had a head on her shoulders.

"He's five months old," Smitty told his mother.

"Then that's one expense we'd have to stand. Of course, it *is* cheaper for a male than a female."

Male? Female? Who'd checked? Not Anthony.

Smitty placed the kitten on the floor, rolled him over on his back and rubbed his belly. Anthony took a good look and restrained a sigh of relief. Sincere was definitely a He.

Smitty's sister was down on the floor, examining the cat now. "Hey, Mom, he's cross-eyed."

Three pairs of Smithson eyes fixed on Sincere. "Oh, my, he really is," Smitty's mother said. "Do you suppose he can see all right?"

Hildy spoke up quickly. "Better than most cats, because he can see two ways at once."

Why Mrs. Smithson started to laugh, Anthony couldn't understand. Hildy's answer sounded reasonable enough to him.

The woman said, "Well, he's awfully cute anyhow. And we've been thinking about getting another cat."

"Then you'll take him?" Anthony and Hildy both said at once.

"If you're sure it's all right with your parents."

"Tony's in my room at school," Smitty said.

"Then, of course, that makes it all right with their parents," his mother said.

Anthony had to think that one over.

Hildy said, "My dad knows we're trying to find him a home. He told us we had to get rid of him right now—today."

Mrs. Smithson's eyes swept from Hildy to Anthony. She smiled. "Wrap him up. We'll take him."

"Hooray!" Smitty said. His sister jumped up and down, to Sincere's consternation, and clapped her hands. Hildy and Anthony traded smiles of relief.

"Norrie," Mrs. Smithson said to her daughter, "go out to the garage and see if you can find Toughy's old sandbox. We'll have to keep the kitten inside until he knows this is his home."

"Okay." Norrie ran for the back door, then stopped and whipped around as if she'd remembered something important. "You both can come back and play with him any time you want to."

"We hope you *will*," her mother said to them.

Hildy spoke for both her and Anthony. "We'd really adore that."

"Good."

As Norrie disappeared out the door, Smitty asked, "What's his name?"

"Sincere."

"Sincere?" Smitty made a face. "Where'd you ever get a name like that?"

Hildy glared at him. "It's a perfectly good name. What's wrong with it?"

Smitty's mother said, "It's a darling name. We couldn't have come up with anything nearly that cute."

Smitty shrugged. "I can always call him Sin. That's not so bad."

Anthony could tell Hildy didn't think much of that.

Smitty's mother said, "You'll call him by his proper name. That's what he's used to."

Hildy's eyes, triumphant now, transfixed Smitty. So there!

After a moment, he grinned at her. "A rose by any other name—"

Sincere chose that moment to let out a raucous cry.

"—would never meow that sweet," Smitty's mother finished and they all laughed.

When the laughter died, Anthony said, "Well, I guess we'd better go."

When they started to leave, in a room that opened off the kitchen, he noticed newspapers spread over a table. But the important thing was not the newspapers but what sat on them. "Hey, that's a P–51," he exclaimed.

"P–51D," Smitty said. "You interested in models?"

"I'm building a P–51 right now, 1/72 scale. It looks like a midget compared to that. That's really something."

"It's a control-line model, sixteen-inch wing span. My dad and I fly it."

"No kidding?"

"Yeah. Come on in and take a look."

Anthony and Hildy followed Smitty into what was obviously a dining room. Then Anthony saw that the wing of the plane seemed to be broken off. It was lying on the table. "What happened to the wing?" he asked, concerned.

"Oh, that." Smitty picked it up and ran his fingers along the trailing edge. "Well, I had a little crack-up. A gust of wind got me. I should have given it a little more up elevator, but I didn't. So pow!"

Anthony assumed the plane was ruined. "Too bad." He shook his head sympathetically.

"Oh, it isn't anything. It's made for that. When you crash, the wings and fuselage are made to drop off. You can put them back together easy enough."

"I'm sure glad to hear that." Anthony lightly touched the plane's surface. "Nice finish."

"Why is it such a funny color?" Hildy asked.

"That's camouflage olive drab. That's how they painted them in World War II," Smitty told her.

"Well, anyhow the red nose is pretty."

Anthony corrected her. "Red spinner." He asked Smitty, "Did you build the model or buy it?"

"Bought it. I started on the PT–19 trainer. That's the one to learn on. A while back I began having troubles with the engine. My dad took it apart and put it back together again. After that it wouldn't work at all, so he let me buy this one."

"Do they cost much?"

"About ten dollars in discount stores. Why? You thinking of getting one? If you do you can come out with my dad and me when we fly."

Anthony thought of his money box. "I'd sure like to. But I don't know—I'd have to think about it."

"Hey, I got an idea," Smitty said, then stopped himself. "But I guess I'd better ask my dad first."

Anthony never did find out what Smitty's idea was. As he and Hildy set out for home, she said, "Think you'll get one?"

"I guess not—ten dollars is a lot of money."

"It sure is." Then she sighed and changed the subject. "I wish we could have kept Sincere."

"Me, too. He was a nice cat." Anthony was quiet for a time, then he began to chuckle. "Boy, I felt like I was getting the third degree when Mrs. Smithson was asking all those questions. How'd you know a cat had to be eight months old before you could get him fixed?"

"I didn't."

"You didn't?"

"No." She was thoughtful for a moment. "Seems like I might have heard it someplace though. But I figure when people ask a question, all they want is an answer. And most times they don't remember what you told them anyhow, just that you told them."

Anthony wasn't quite sure he agreed with that philosophy, but, on the other hand, as his dad used to say, you had to have some smarts to even come up with it.

"You think Sincere will have a good home?" she asked.

"Oh, sure."

"How can you tell?"

Anthony had to put his own head to work this time. "It's hard to say—but I think he will. You know why?"

"Why?"

"Because they act like they really want him."

His answer seemed to satisfy her. As they walked along, Anthony suddenly realized that not once that afternoon had he felt like a shrimp. When they reached home, he left her to race up to his room, grab a pencil and ruler, and measure himself against the mark on the closet door. Sure enough. Maybe he had strained for it a little, but there was no doubt he was taller, no doubt he was starting to shoot up. Almost a half inch!

9

A Secret Mission

Anthony sat across from Ms. Honeycott, spreading his knees wide apart, then batting them together.

The true-blues glinted with amusement as she watched him. Finally she said, "What's this I hear about you helping Hildy with her math homework?"

He stretched his arms far above him, clasped his hands and rested them on his head. "Well, she helps *me* with English. She's good in English and I'm good in math, so we trade."

"I thought you said you couldn't stand the girl."

"Who, Hildy?"

"Yes, Hildy."

He looked at her with an expression that said, Where did you ever get that idea? Then he shrugged. "Hildy's okay—when you get to know her." And Anthony was getting to know her much better. He really enjoyed her company now. Once in a while though she was still a pain. Especially if he messed around when she was helping him with English. Then she drew on her supply of big words, most of them sarcastic, to let him know he was a dumb ignoramus. That was her worst fault. She said what she thought without considering other people's feelings. But she had a good side, too. She listened. Now he had someone to talk to about his dad. And she was interested. When he'd made her understand what a really great guy his dad was, she put her mind to work trying to figure out what had happened to him.

"You know what I think?" she said. "I think he's found an important job—a really important job. No, a *vitally* important job."

"*Vitally* important?"

"*Vitally* important."

Vitally important sounded about as important as you could get. "Then how come I don't hear from him?"

"Now wait a minute—I'm thinking. Does *he* speak a foreign language?"

Anthony couldn't imagine what she had in mind. "I guess maybe he took Spanish in school. Sometimes when we'd go to a Mexican restaurant, he'd kid around with the waitresses. He'd say, 'Muchas gracias,' and stuff like that."

Hildy nodded wisely. "Then that's it."

"What's it?"

"The government sent him on this secret mission—probably to some Latin American country. He had to leave in a hurry, and they wouldn't let him communicate with anybody. That's how they do it on television. And *they* take from real life, you know."

"Yeah," Anthony said thoughtfully. "Yeah. That makes a lot of sense. It's got to be something like that. That's why I haven't heard. Boy, I hope he's all right. . . . I guess he can take care of himself though."

After that Anthony had felt much better. Still that wasn't the kind of story he cared to try on Ms. Honeycott now. But then, if it was a secret mission, he should keep it to himself anyhow. "Yeah, Hildy's okay," he said.

Ms. Honeycott said, "Most people *are* when you get to know them better."

Anthony thought that over, then leaned forward, put his elbows on her desk, rested his face in his hands, and changed the subject. "You remember me telling you about this kid, Smitty, the one who took the Siamese cat?"

"Yes, I do."

"Well, he gave me his old control-line model. His dad said he could. His dad said it was the least they could do for giving them a nice cat like Sincere. They gave Hildy a tote bag. She said she was thrilled." And it took plenty to thrill Hildy.

"What's a control-line model?"

Anthony explained, then said, "This one's a PT–19 trainer, twenty-two-inch wing span."

"Have you flown it yet?"

"No, not yet. Something's wrong with the engine."

"That doesn't sound like much of a gift if it's broken."

To Anthony, broken or not, it was a magnificent gift. For days he had kept it in his room simply to admire. "There's hardly a scratch on it. And the engine—well, that just needs fixing."

"Maybe Mr. Diamond can fix it for you."

"Maybe." Anthony doubted it. Mr. Diamond had come home from work one night to find Anthony out on the back porch, fooling with the plane.

Although he'd had little to say to Anthony since their Little League days, when his eyes lit on the trainer, he said, "Watcha got there?"

Anthony thought it best not to mention the cat. He told him what it was and said, "Smitty, a kid in my room at school, gave it to me. It's broken, but he says if I can fix it, I can go out with him and his dad and learn to fly it."

Mr. Diamond sat down on the porch steps and examined the model. Sounding like a doctor, he said, "What seems to be the problem?"

"It's the engine."

"The engine, huh. Well, I imagine I can do something about that."

"You can?" Anthony couldn't hide the surprise in his voice.

"I don't see why not. Working in the parts department the way I do, you might say I'm around engines all day. And in the Navy I was a machinist's mate. I guess I know a thing or two by now. After supper I'll take a look at it."

"That's great." Anthony had thought of buying a new engine, but this was even better. The idea of taking anything from his money box still had no appeal for him.

After a quick supper, Mr. Diamond read the instructions that went with the model. Then he took the engine apart, put it back together again, drove down to the hobby shop for fuel, came back, gassed up in the backyard, turned the prop a few times, hooked the battery to the glow plug, said, "Here goes," and gave the propeller a good spin. Not a whimper. He scowled. "Can't understand that."

He fiddled with the fuel mixture, and tried again. And again. And again. Still nothing. After a few more tries, he began to grow a little red in the face. "Something mighty wrong here, Tony. Don't know if it can be fixed. That's the cheap stuff they turn out these days. Nothing works. Well, I can't do any more on it tonight. Don't have the proper tools here. I'll take it in to the garage and play with it."

That was three days ago. Now Anthony said to Ms. Honeycott, "He took it to work to fix it, but he hasn't said anything so I guess he can't."

"Don't worry. If it can be fixed, any automobile mechanic should be able to do it."

"But he's no automobile mechanic."

"No, but there are enough of them in a garage. He'll probably ask one of them to take a look at it."

"You think so?"

"Oh, I'm sure of it."

And she was right. At least about the engine getting fixed. That same night Mr. Diamond brought it home and said, "Well, I found our trouble, all right. Some bonehead must have taken the thing apart and put it back together with the piston turned around 180 degrees."

Anthony wondered who that could have been. "Does it work now?"

"You bet it works. Come outside and I'll show you."

In the backyard, Mr. Diamond put fuel in the exhaust, cranked the prop, then hooked everything up. Anthony squatted close to watch. On the third spin of the prop, the engine caught, and the roar almost blasted him off his haunches.

Mr. Diamond shouted above the din. "How about *that*, fella?"

Anthony, all excited now, shouted back, "That's really great."

Mr. Diamond cut the engine and the noise faded away. "I told you with the proper tools I'd get it working. You remember that, Tony, that's all it takes, the proper tools."

"Now I'll be able to go out with Smitty and his dad."

"Oh? Where do they go?"

"Mostly to that place they call an industrial park—where all those new factories are. On Saturdays and Sundays there's no one there so they use the parking lots."

"The industrial park, huh. Well, that's not far. All right. Tell you what we'll do. Saturday morning we'll go over and give it a try."

"Oh." The word came out flat. Anthony very much wanted to fly the trainer but memories of Little League gave him mixed emotions about trying it with Mr. Diamond.

The following afternoon, to Anthony's distress, old Mrs. Puckett thrust another letter at him and, with it, a dollar bill. "You get me some stamps, boy. Put one on the letter and mail it. Bring the rest back to me. Don't you tell nobody."

Not knowing what else to do, Anthony shoved the envelope and the money in a pocket and left the house. He walked over to the shopping center, bought the stamps, returned home and gave all but one to the old woman. She never even counted. "You're a good boy," she said. "I'll tell Edgar Doyle about you when he comes. He's got a good heart, Edgar Doyle has. He'll see you get rewarded."

Anthony could only nod. As he watched her shuffle back to her room, he felt sad. Then he looked for Mrs. Diamond, found her in the kitchen and handed her the envelope and the extra stamp. "She gave me another letter and had me buy some stamps."

Mrs. Diamond glanced at the name and address and shook her head. "Poor Ma."

"She always keeps talking about how nice your brother is."

"Oh, he's nice all right. He's just as nice as he can be when he wants something. He sweet-talked Ma right out of all the money she had in the world—her life savings. And now she doesn't even remember."

All the money she had in the world? Anthony visualized his money box empty. "How could you forget something like that? I mean, how could you think somebody was good when they did something bad?"

"I don't know, Tony. When you love someone, it's real easy to fool yourself and make believe they're the way you want them to be. I just guess it's easier for Ma that way." She ripped up the envelope and threw it in the kitchen trash pail. "Don't you worry about the letter. She'll never even remember she wrote it." She gave a deep sigh. "I wish she *could* write to him. I mean, with him not minding. Most of all, I wish *he'd* write to her. But I guess we can't always get people to act the way we want."

"I guess," Anthony said.

As soon as he left the kitchen, he ran upstairs and, although he realized it was silly, checked his money box, counted every penny. It was all there just as he knew it would be. Yet he couldn't quite shake the feeling that he was destitute.

10

The Wild Blue Yonder

On Saturday morning Anthony said to Hildy, "You want to go with us to fly the trainer? We could ask your dad."

"No. Airplanes don't thrill me that much. Maybe someday Mom will take me over and we'll watch for a while."

Anthony was secretly glad. He wasn't quite sure of what it took to fly a control-line model, and he had no wish to make a fool of himself in front of Hildy. Besides, if Smitty was there, they'd have plenty to talk about. At school, they talked airplanes all lunch hour. When Hildy was with them, she soon grew bored and moved off to join someone else.

That morning Mr. Diamond wanted to get an early start. He poured over the flight instructions at the breakfast table, then loaded everything securely in the car. As they were about to set out, he remembered he had left the instructions in the house and sent Anthony back for them.

Anthony was in the kitchen when the phone rang. He snatched the paper from the table and ran out to the hall to answer. Hildy had already taken the call. He heard her say, "My brother?" There was a slight pause, then, "I think he's gone. Let me take a look."

Her brother? Hildy didn't have a brother.

When she turned from the phone and saw him, she said, "Oh, Tony—it's for you—Smitty."

"For me?" he said stupidly. Then *he* was Hildy's brother. Of course Smitty would have thought so. Hildy was in a different room at school so he'd never heard her last name. But Hildy herself had reacted to the idea so naturally.

When he answered the phone, Smitty said, "I was afraid I'd missed you. Your sister thought you were gone."

"Yeah, well—" He glanced around to make sure Hildy had disappeared. "My—my sister didn't know." The word felt strange yet pleasant on his tongue.

Smitty had called to let Anthony know he wouldn't see him that morning. He and his dad had to run some important errands, it seemed.

"That's sure too bad," Anthony said, but when he hung up, he felt relieved. You never knew how Mr. Diamond was going to act with other people. And then there was that different name business, Diamond and Lang. Who wanted to make explanations?

He joined Mr. Diamond and they took off for the industrial park, an area of attractive, handsomely landscaped buildings devoted to light manufacturing. As Smitty had previously suggested, they used the largest parking lot. Mr. Diamond, well acquainted with the written instructions now, set the trainer on the ground and placed the battery alongside. With his tongue, he wet a finger, then held it into the air. "Look at that—no wind to contend with. I tell you, there's nothing like getting an early start. We've got the whole place to ourselves, too."

He stretched the guide lines along the ground as far as they would reach and positioned the attached handle. "Now you watch everything I do, Tony. First, we'll give 'er a little gas." He squirted fuel into the exhaust, then cranked the prop over a few times. Anthony took it all in, trying to commit the routine to memory.

Mr. Diamond hooked wires from the battery to the glow plug on the engine. "While I turn the prop, you hang on to the plane—tight. When the engine catches, I'll disconnect the battery leads." He glanced at the instruction sheet and read, " 'To adjust mixture, turn needle valve until engine runs smoothly.' All right, when I say we're ready, I'll hold the plane. You run back and grab the handle. And remember everything I told you."

Anthony, a little nervous now, nodded.

Mr. Diamond spun the prop. The engine made a *putt-putt* sound and died. After several tries, it finally caught with a weak *plup-plup plup-plup*. He played with the needle valve until a steady whine set up. "That's got it."

As firmly as Anthony held it, the plane seemed to have a life of its own. He felt as if it were trying to break away from him. When Mr. Diamond took it, Anthony raced over, snatched up the handle, slid his hand inside to find the finger grooves, and tested. He pulled the top toward him and the elevators went up, the bottom toward him and the elevators went down, just as they were supposed to. Easy enough so far.

Mr. Diamond shouted above the engine noise, "Get ready, Tony. I'm letting go." He released the plane and off it shot. Quickly, he ran over to join Anthony.

Anthony, trying to hold the lines taut, gave a slight pull on the handle and the trainer began to climb. "It's flying," he yelled, all excited now. He began to turn with it in a circle as the plane, perhaps eight feet off the ground, whizzed around. Now it was no longer easy. He found himself overcontrolling, working the handle too hard, too much. The plane started porpoising through the air.

"No, no, no," Mr. Diamond yelled. "Give 'er a little up elevator. Too much. Down elevator. Too much."

Up, down, nothing seemed to work.

"Get it into neutral and keep it level."

But where was neutral? Somewhere between up and down. "I'm dizzy," Anthony said.

Mr. Diamond grasped Anthony's shoulder to steady

him. In a moment, the engine sputtered and died.

"Easy does it—bring it in for a landing."

Now everything was happening too fast for Anthony. Suddenly the words, "Don't forget the up elevator!" blasted against his eardrums. He jerked the handle up toward him. Too much. Too hard. Too soon. In the next instant, the plane stalled and crashed to the ground. Anthony stood there, staring at the scattered pieces. He could have cried. Then he remembered the model was made for crashes.

Mr. Diamond scowled. "You've got to do better than that or we'll be spending all our time putting the thing together."

"It's tricky," Anthony said.

"Can't be that hard. I'll have the next go at it and show you how it's done."

When they reassembled the plane and had it running again, Anthony held it while Mr. Diamond scurried over to grab the handle and test. Up elevator. Down elevator. "Let 'er go," he called.

Anthony took his hands from the plane and immediately it started to climb. When it was well off the ground, Mr. Diamond began turning. "You see that, Tony," he shouted, "nothing to it. All you've got to—" The plane began an erratic up and down flight. Each time he tried to correct he overdid.

Anthony felt like laughing. But he didn't. He wanted to shout, "Give 'er a little up elevator. Down elevator. Too much." But he didn't.

Mr. Diamond fought the thing, his face growing redder by the second. Then suddenly, whether by accident or design, he happened on the right position and, for a few moments, the plane settled, straight and level, on its circular course. Then the engine died. He brought the trainer in with a *plop* that again left a bunch of pieces on the ground.

Anthony smiled to himself but said, "You got it going pretty good there toward the last."

"Well, I was just getting the feel of it. Going to take a little practice though. Some real skill involved here, I can see that. I'll give it another run or two—just to get the hang of it. That way I'll be able to show you better."

Rather than one or two runs, it was closer to a half dozen. Each time, Anthony helped pick up the pieces and put the plane back together. But Mr. Diamond wasn't about to let any mechanical toy defeat him. Finally he managed one fairly good flight, bringing the plane down with a *bumpety-bump* but all in one piece.

"A lot of skill involved here, Tony—a *lot* of skill." Mr. Diamond's eyes fastened on the trainer. "I thought it was a kid's game, but I can see there's more to it than that—a lot more. Makes it interesting though. Yes, sir."

Anthony could tell that Mr. Diamond was thoroughly intrigued. Now I'll never get a chance at it, he thought. But he was wrong. At that point, a few other people started to arrive with models. Mr. Diamond said, "You take over now, Tony. I'll help you." Anthony suspected that, before he performed before an audience, Mr. Diamond was determined to gain a lot more of all that skill he saw involved there.

While Anthony flew the plane, Mr. Diamond, in full stride, shouted orders. Up elevator. Down elevator. Neutral. Instead of making him nervous, Anthony thought it funny. The man was like a big kid and showing all the signs of the budding enthusiast.

Between flights, he critically examined the planes of other flyers. As two teenagers, one with a Sopwith Camel, the other with a Fokker D–VII, fought a mock dogfight, he stood, arms folded, watching through his thick glasses. When the planes climbed, looped, and dived at each other, his head climbed, looped, and dived with them. "Yes, sir, a lot of skill involved here," he said.

He struck up a conversation with a man whose son was not much more experienced than Anthony. Anthony heard Mr. Diamond say, "My boy's just starting—first solo flight, you might say. I figure, let him chalk up a few hours on the trainer, then we'll get him something that really goes."

Anthony decided that was only talk, Mr. Diamond, as usual, practicing his one-upmanship. Much to his surprise, when their fuel ran out and they started for home, Mr. Diamond said, "Tell you what we'll do. We'll go back to the house and get us a bite to eat. Then we'll hop in the car and take in a couple of hobby shops. Might as well get a line on what's available in this stuff."

Before the afternoon was over, to Anthony's astonishment, he was the possessor of not one but two flying models. He felt as if he were on his way to owning his own air force. No, not his own. Mr. Diamond was in this thing, too. In it body and soul, it seemed. He'd been torn between the choice of a P–40 Warhawk or a Ju 87D Stuka, a sleek plane, complete with sliding front and rear canopies, a bomb that dropped, and rear-mounted machine gun. When the clerk said, "It takes a third guide line to release that bomb. It's a real skill-tester," that did it.

Mr. Diamond said, "Well, what do you think, Tony?"

Anthony was too overwhelmed to know what he thought. "I don't know. What do you think?"

"I think skill-testing is the name of the game, that's what I think. After all, we don't want to fool around with that beginner's stuff for too long."

So the Stuka it was. And "we" owned it.

Early Sunday morning, before church and in an empty parking lot, they were out skill-testing, Mr. Diamond very nearly cracking up the Stuka now.

After one particularly disastrous landing, Anthony said, "Well, they say any landing's a good one if you can walk away from it."

"Huh?" In another moment, to Anthony's surprise, Mr. Diamond let out a guffaw that turned into a real belly laugh and wound down to a chuckle. He slapped

Anthony on the back. "That's pretty good, Tony—pretty good."

Anthony thought so, too.

"You know, Tony, all this stuff takes is practice and a steady hand. We'll get it licked yet. Before you know it, we'll be doing aerobatics with the best of them."

"I hope so."

"Sure we will. You know, I been thinking. There's a hobby show over in Anaheim next weekend. Maybe we should go. I understand they'll have plenty of models and all kinds of other crafts. Something for everybody, you might say. We'll take Mom and Hildy along, too."

"That sounds great," Anthony said. "I bet they'd really like something like that."

As it turned out, Mom and Hildy weren't crazy about poking into every stall that held a model airplane or an engine. They went off by themselves to see the crafts displays. Anthony and Mr. Diamond spent the afternoon collecting literature on all the aircraft in the show. When the loudspeaker announced flying demonstrations in the parking lot, they went outside to find radio-control models performing.

"Look at that," Mr. Diamond said, "no guide lines—nothing."

"That's really something," Anthony agreed.

Some of the little planes soared high into the air to go through all kinds of aerobatics, then zoom in for three-point landings. Others put on simulated World

War I dogfights. After that, another group whizzed around a pylon for an exciting air race. It seemed only minutes before it was time to meet Hildy and Mom at the hot dog stand.

By then, they were all hungry. But so was everyone else at the show. People stood in long lines waiting to buy refreshments.

Mr. Diamond said, "Well, it's easy to see we'll never get waited on here. Tell you what—why don't we all pile in the car and, on the way home, stop for pizza."

"Oh, goody," Hildy exclaimed. "I love pizza. In fact, I adore it."

"Me, too," Anthony said.

Mr. Diamond said, "How about you, Mom?"

"As long as Mrs. Stubbins next door is watching Ma, it's fine with me."

So they piled in the car, Mom and Hildy in the back seat, Anthony, gripping a plastic bag full of exciting pamphlets, in front with Mr. Diamond.

As Mr. Diamond pointed the nose of the car toward home, he said, "You know, Tony, I'm really impressed with that radio-control flying we saw—*really* impressed."

"Me, too." Anthony decided he'd have to be rich before he could ever afford anything like that. You could easily spend a few hundred dollars.

"A lot of skill involved there. Yes, sir, a *lot* of skill." Mr. Diamond was quiet for a moment. Then he said, "You know, that just might be the way to go."

Wow!

11

Code Name: Ethel

Anthony hung up the phone and went looking for Hildy. He found her curled up in a chair watching television in her grandmother's room. The old woman rested against the pillows of her bed and stared into space. As he poked his head in the door, Hildy took her eyes from the screen long enough to say, "There's an old western on. You want to watch?"

"Sure." Mrs. Puckett had long ceased to hold any terror for him. Perhaps that was because Hildy treated her with the tolerance of an older child for a younger, sometimes growing impatient with her, sometimes mothering her and acting fiercely protective. Whether she received a scolding or a hugging, the old woman seemed equally pleased, as if all she craved was attention. Often these days, Anthony joined the two of them. The room always smelled of liniment. That had bothered him at first. Now he was getting used to it.

He pulled up a chair near Hildy's and tilted it back

against the wall. On the screen, the delicate hands of a pretty young woman fluttered to her throat as a slick-haired cowboy said, "Ma'am, running a ranch is no job for a lady."

"Is that the good guy or the bad guy?" Anthony asked.

"The bad guy, of course."

As the camera focused on the man's face, Anthony said, "Oh, sure. He's got a mustache and he needs a shave. If he'd had his hat on, I'd have known right off."

"Sshh," Hildy said.

Anthony closed his mouth. There were two things on television Hildy took very seriously, old movies and baseball games. Anthony enjoyed them, too, but he also liked to talk. She was always shushing him. Well, if she was going to do that, she'd just have to wait to hear about the terrific surprise he had for her. Although it had nearly killed him, he'd kept it to himself for three days, waiting until he was sure.

On Sunday, while they were out flying, Mr. Diamond had said, "I been thinking. Maybe one of these weekends we should take a day off."

That didn't sound like the man at all. Every chance he had he was out practicing with Anthony, the two of them improving their skill steadily. "You mean, spend a day going around pricing radio-control again?"

"No. I mean, how about me getting tickets for Dodger Stadium? We'll take in one of the games."

Anthony could hardly contain himself. Although he no longer played anything but scrub baseball in the schoolyard, he had developed a genuine interest in the sport. So had Hildy. They followed all the big and minor league games on television. "That would be great," he said. "Hildy will really be thrilled."

"Hildy?"

"Sure, she adores baseball," Anthony said, using her words. "She watches it all the time on television —knows a lot about it."

"Oh, yes—well—I don't know—"

It was clear Mr. Diamond had never given a thought to including Hildy. Worried now, Anthony said, "She'd really be sick if she missed something like that."

"Yes, well—" Mr. Diamond rubbed his chin and took a moment to seriously consider the matter. At length he said, "Well, let me see if I can get three tickets. If I can, we'll take Hildy. But she'd better not fuss to go home before the game's over or make a nuisance of herself."

"Hildy wouldn't do anything like that. She really adores baseball."

And now it was settled. Mr. Diamond had told Anthony on the phone, only minutes earlier, that he'd bought three tickets.

As a commercial flashed on the screen, Anthony, permitted to talk now, decided to tease Hildy with his news. "I know something you don't know." He began to rock back and forth in his chair.

"What?"

"Something."

"Like what?"

"Like something you're going to get to do—a surprise."

"Tell me."

"Later—I'm watching the commercial." He continued to rock his chair, eyes on the screen instead of on her.

"No, tell me now." Hildy, obviously curious, grabbed the chair to get his attention.

He lost his balance and toppled against the bed. The old woman let out a moan. "Oh, I'm sorry," he said, fully aware by now that any sudden bounce of the bed gave her pain.

As he carefully righted the chair, she jockeyed herself into a sitting position and turned a disgruntled eye on him. "What you up to, boy? You aiming to give me another bad spell?"

"Honest, Mrs. Puckett, I didn't mean—"

Before he'd finished the sentence, Hildy was at her grandmother's side, easing her back against the pillows. "Tony didn't mean to hurt you, Gran. It was my fault he fell." She took her grandmother's frail hand and rubbed it between her own, explaining to Anthony, "She likes that. It warms her hands." Talking above a cat-food commercial, she said, "And Gran, you stop calling him 'boy.' His name is Tony."

"Eh?" her grandmother said although there was nothing wrong with her hearing.

Hildy pointed to Anthony. "His name is Tony."

The old woman peered at him. "Tony?"

"Yes, Tony."

"I know'd a Tony once—Eyetalian fella. You Eye-talian, boy?"

Hildy shook her head hopelessly and Anthony had to smile. She said, "Maybe if you'd start calling her Gran, she'd start calling you Tony."

Anthony had never considered that possibility. But why not? He decided if he made a joke of it, it would be easier. He went over to the bed, careful not to touch it. For Hildy's benefit, he said to the old woman, "Me Tony. You Gran. Okay?"

She looked as if she didn't understand. Like a child, she parroted, "Me Tony. You Gran—" which sent Anthony and Hildy into paroxysms of laughter. The old woman caught the mood and started to chuckle along with them.

When the laughter subsided, Hildy said, "And *me* Tarzan," which started the whole thing all over.

For some reason, Anthony glanced over to the door to find Mrs. Diamond standing there watching them, a curious expression on her face. "Tony, come out here a minute," she said.

As she stepped into the hall, he followed, puzzled by her manner. She closed the door of her mother's room. Even in the dim light of the corridor, her smile seemed forced. "You three make enough racket to wake the dead."

He knew she had not called him out to chide him for

that. It was not her way. He stood there awkwardly waiting, feeling uneasy. Finally she said, "I've got a real big surprise for you."

Still he felt uneasy. Still he said nothing.

"Someone's come to see you."

Someone? Who would come to see him? Not . . . He said, "Ms. Honeycott, I bet."

"No, it's your dad."

"My dad!"

"Yes."

"Where is he?"

"In the front room. And, Tony, when you see him, ask—"

He never heard what he was supposed to ask. He flew through the hall, tore into the living room, and without stopping to look at the man, threw his arms around him and hugged him for all he was worth. "Oh, boy, am I ever glad to see you," he said, choking a little on the words.

His dad hugged him back. "Here, let me get a glimpse at you." He grasped Anthony's shoulders to ease him back. "Look at you—you've grown so much I wouldn't know you."

"Almost an inch." Well, maybe he was exaggerating, but not much. He had so many questions to ask he hardly knew where to begin. He blurted, "Did you see Ms. Honeycott? Did you get everything fixed?"

"Ms. Honeycott?"

"The caseworker."

"Oh. Well, no, I didn't." When Anthony looked at him with a perplexed expression, he added, "Not yet."

"Then how did you know where to find me?"

"I got in touch with the Sauters. They gave me this address."

Of course. It seemed a million years ago that his dad had left him with the Sauters. But surely they must have given him the name of the agency. Why hadn't he gone there to fix things? Anthony decided he simply wasn't thinking straight. Naturally his dad would want to see him first. They could go together to talk to Ms. Honeycott. He wondered now if the agency would let him leave the Diamonds immediately. The Diamonds! He had never given them a thought. Mr. Diamond and the Stuka. Would he fly it alone? And Hildy—he hadn't even told her about Dodger Stadium. And there were those three tickets. . . .

He pushed the disturbing thoughts to the back of his head as his father took a seat on the couch and said, "Sit down, son. I want to hear all about you."

Anthony drew up a chair to face him. He wanted to drink in the sight of his dad and refresh his memory of him. After all there was no rush. And they had a lot of catching up to do. "You sure look good," Anthony said. He might have added, "to me," because that was closer to the truth. His father looked far from good, thinner and paler than Anthony remembered, and eyes more bloodshot.

"And you look about as healthy as a vitamin." In a

gesture almost painfully familiar to Anthony, his father ran his fingers through heavy, brown hair. But less familiar and more painful to see was the tremor in his hands. "I'll bet you're getting a lot of good food."

"Oh, sure. Mrs. Diamond's a great cook." His father's appearance worried Anthony, but he consoled himself with the thought that if his dad had been on a secret mission, there was no telling what he'd gone through. "That's a neat suit. I don't remember that one."

"It's new."

That had to mean something good. You couldn't buy a suit without money. "I bet you've got a really important job now." He was going to say *vitally* important, but he didn't want to embarrass his dad if that wasn't quite the case.

"It's a job," his father said with a rueful smile.

"Secret maybe? You can't talk about it?"

To Anthony's surprise, his father frowned. "What's that supposed to mean?"

"I mean, like if you were working for the government or something they wouldn't let you talk about it."

His father gave a derisive laugh. "I'm certainly not working for the government."

"A big corporation maybe?"

"No."

"Who then?"

"You're full of questions, aren't you? What difference does it make where I work?"

"Well, none, I suppose," Anthony said, taken aback. "I just wanted to be sure you were doing okay."

There was a long moment of silence. Finally his father said, "Well, I guess there's no reason why I can't tell you this much—I'm working in a motel."

Anthony couldn't hide the disappointment in his voice. "A motel?"

"Yes, a motel."

"What do you do?"

His father regarded him doubtfully, then in a flat voice said, "I know the woman who owns the place. She offered me the job of manager."

"Oh, manager—well, manager sounds pretty good." Anthony tried to visualize himself living in a motel. Maybe it wouldn't be so bad. Couldn't be any worse than some of the other places they'd lived in. It seemed strange though—his father, an engineer, working as a motel manager. "How come the woman gave *you* the job?"

A look of annoyance spread over his father's face. "Look, I got the job—that's all you need to know." When he saw the hurt in Anthony's eyes, his voice softened. "Look, son, I didn't mean to sound—" He broke off and started again. "It's like this—Ethel, the woman who owns the place—well, we had a few things in common. She thought she could help me out—just until I got settled. You understand?"

Anthony nodded because he felt that was what his father expected of him. He wanted to ask what his dad had in common with the woman Ethel. Then a sudden fear touched him. He remembered another woman. His father used to come home from her house smelling of something that Anthony soon came to recognize as liquor. He pushed the thought away quickly. "Where is it?"

"Where is what?"

"The motel."

Again his father looked at Anthony doubtfully. "Up north."

"Northern California?"

His father pulled a pack of cigarettes from his pocket and glanced around, obviously looking for an ashtray. Anthony sprang to his feet to get the only thing in the room that seemed at all suitable for cigarettes, a small, fluted glass dish. He handed it to his father who glanced at it, set it on the table near the couch, then absently stuffed the pack of cigarettes back into his pocket.

"Northern California?" Anthony asked again.

"What are you talking about?"

Anthony could see his father had already forgotten. "Is the motel in Northern California?"

With a sudden spurt of irritation, his father said, "Now, look, what is this? The third degree?"

Anthony lapsed into an uneasy silence. He had forgotten how touchy his father sometimes was. But why would anyone be touchy about something like that? Finally he said, "You want to see Ms. Honeycott today? I'll go with you."

"Who?"

"Ms. Honeycott, the caseworker."

"Oh. Well, not today. I don't have the time."

"But, Dad, you don't know all the red tape agencies make you go through. It'll take forever if we don't get started."

"I'm not reading you."

"Well, before I can come to live with you, we'll have to get permission from the agency."

His father stared at him blankly, then said, "You thought I—" He ran his fingers nervously through his hair again. "Why, you can't live in a motel. A motel is no place for kids. Not this one anyhow. Even Ethel doesn't have her own girl there."

Anthony could feel a cold chill creep inside him and settle in the pit of his stomach like a rock of ice. "Where's *her* girl?"

"With her grandmother."

Anthony had no grandmother. "Where's her husband?"

"She's divorced."

"You going to marry her?"

"What is this? The third degree again?" His father got up and started pacing the room. "I knew it was a mistake to come here."

Anthony closed his mouth. A nerve in his cheek worked as he sat there glowering at his feet, the icy rock slowly turning him to stone.

His father stopped pacing and faced him. "Now,

look, son, it's not that I don't want you with me—you know better than that, don't you?" When Anthony said nothing, he went on. "It just isn't possible right now." Again he waited for some response from Anthony. Nothing. "You kids—you just can't understand—" Again nothing. "Why do you think I came here? I had to see that you were all right—had to see with my own eyes that you were with decent people—that you were happy."

Now Anthony said, "Took you long enough."

His father stared at him for a long moment, then, in an injured tone, said, "You know I would have made it sooner if I'd been able. Try to understand—I've had problems."

Relentless, Anthony said, "What problems?"

A shadow passed over his father's face. "Ethel's right. There's no way kids can understand about the world until they have to face it themselves." In a self-pitying tone, he added, "I've had to take more than my share of hard knocks." His voice rose. "More than my share. There's just so much a man can stand." He stared at Anthony, his face all hollows, his body sagging beneath the new suit.

For a moment, Anthony had wanted to hate the man. Then an overwhelming rush of love and pity swept through him. When he found his voice, all he could say was, "I'm glad you came, Dad."

The tension lifted from his father's face. "That's more like it." He sat down on the couch again. "Now I want to hear all about *you*. Are you happy here? Seems like a comfortable house."

"Sure, Dad, it's great."

"Do you like the people? Are they treating you well?"

"Yes, sure."

"Mrs. Diamond seems like a nice woman. I wish I had time to stick around and meet her husband. Maybe next time."

"You coming back?"

"Well, of course."

"When?"

His father shifted uneasily in his seat. Avoiding Anthony's eyes, he said, "Well, I don't know exactly when. You know, there's a lot of work in a motel—long hours—ties you up quite a bit." When Anthony said nothing, he glanced around the room and said again, "Seems like a comfortable house." After a moment he looked anxiously into Anthony's face. "You *are* happy here?"

"Oh, sure, Dad. I've got my own room—it's great. And then there's Hildy—we get along pretty good— watch television and do homework together, stuff like that. And I'm into control-line models now, me and Mr. Diamond. We fly them. You ought to see how good he's getting—me, too. Boy, that Stuka—you should see that Stuka fly—it's really something. Did I tell you we're going to Dodger Stadium in two weeks? Boy, that's really going to be something. I can hardly—" he broke off when he realized he was babbling.

His father's voice sounded grave. "Sounds as though you're doing all right for yourself."

"Oh, sure, Dad."

"That's all I wanted to know."

After that, they talked for a while about everything that had no real meaning. Then an uncomfortable silence fell. Finally his father glanced at his watch. "Time sure flies when you're having fun," he said with feigned humor, then got to his feet. "I think I'd better be getting back."

"Sure, Dad."

As they walked to the front door, it seemed to Anthony his father's thoughts were already far away. "Do you have a long way to drive?"

Absently, his father said, "Not too far."

The words stabbed. The motel was not in Northern California after all, but in some place called Not Too Far.

His father stood awkwardly at the door for a moment. He started to open it, then had second thoughts. He turned back to Anthony. "You know, I've been keeping my eyes open—looking around all the time. I think things are going to break pretty soon—maybe by fall. I've got a couple of good job possibilities lined up."

"That's great, Dad."

"Of course, I'm not going to take the first thing that falls in my lap."

"No, that wouldn't be any good."

"This time it's got to be a really good job, really secure."

"Sure, Dad."

"As soon as I'm settled—wherever it is—we'll get a house and a housekeeper and line up a school for you. It'll be like old times. How does that sound?"

Anthony opened his mouth but nothing came out.

When he failed to respond, his father repeated, "How does that sound to you?"

Anthony's lips quivered. "Pretty danged good."

His father stared at him strangely. He gave a forced smile, then sent a mock punch to Anthony's chin. In the next moment, Anthony felt himself crushed against his father's chest. Some dim memory inside him caught a faint but familiar smell, something he had failed to notice in his earlier excitement. In the next instant, his father was down the stairs and into the old car Anthony remembered from long ago.

Anthony's voice throbbed as he called after him, "Drive carefully, Dad."

12

The Chinese Puzzle Box

"The Diamonds tell me your dad came to see you," Ms. Honeycott says. "He had no business rushing off like that."

Anthony says, "He had no choice," and gives her an eye-piercing stare.

She says, "You'll notice he came to see you at a time when he could be pretty sure Mr. Diamond would be at work. You'll notice he didn't waste any time hanging around either. He was off before anyone—any adult, that is—could ask where he was living."

"He had no choice," Anthony says.

Ms. Honeycott says, "When a man won't give his address to his own son, I call that pretty irresponsible. No, extremely irresponsible."

"He had no choice," Anthony says.

"He came to see you because he felt guilty, that's all. Once he saw you were in good hands, wham! All he wants is out from under," she says.

Anthony says, "You got it all wrong, Ms. Honeycott."

She says, "And all that business about a house and a housekeeper—well, don't you believe it. Remember what I keep telling you?"

Naturally she's on that reality kick again. Anthony says, "You got it all wrong, Ms. Honeycott."

Ms. Honeycott says, "Don't say I didn't warn you. I told you parents of fosters are always making promises they can't keep. Oh, they mean well enough, and you have to feel sorry for them. They can't always help it if they're not able to pull themselves together. When they can't take charge of their own lives, how can they take charge of their children's?"

He gives her another eye-piercing stare and says, "You got it all wrong, Ms. Honeycott."

This time she answers with what he's been waiting for. "What have I got all wrong?"

"Everything!" Anthony says. He waits a minute to let the sheer force of the dynamite in his voice sink in. And it does. She's all attention now. "I'll tell you what you've got all wrong." He gets up, walks around the room, feeling under tables, running his hand around the windowsill, peering behind the draperies, sneaking up to the door for a surprise attack on the keyhole, his sharp eye making certain no spy lurks on the other side. He can see she's all curiosity now, really impressed.

"I had to be sure there were no bugs," he says. "When important matters are at stake, you just can't be too careful."

"What is it?" Her voice is hushed now and anxious.

"You won't breathe a word of this to anybody?" he asks.

Too overcome to open her mouth, she slowly shakes her head. He sees sincerity in the true-blues.

"I believe you," he says.

"What's it all about?" she asks.

He answers, "I'll tell you what it's all about." He pauses to let the full effect of the words shower over her like a sky rocket. "My dad is a secret agent."

"A secret agent?!" she exclaims.

He hushes her. In a whisper, he says, "Yes. He's on this secret mission for the government. It's very hush-hush. Nobody is supposed to know his whereabouts."

Zap! He can see he's really got her now. The true-blues are blinking like crazy. She says, "I know I shouldn't ask this, but do you know his whereabouts?"

He says quickly, "I can't answer that. I've said too much already. Whereabouts are something the close family never mentions."

"Oh, I see," she says.

He says, "I will say this though, my dad speaks Spanish like a native. That's the only hint I can give you."

Her mouth forms a thoughtful O. "Now I understand," she says. "A fine man like your father would never abandon his boy unless vitally important duties forced him to."

"Now you got it, Ms. Honeycott," Anthony says. "VI-

TALLY important. That's the key word. For the good of the nation."

"For the good of the nation," Ms. Honeycott repeats in reverent tones, and the true-blues look as if they hold all the stars in the American flag.

Anthony says, "When it's all over, my dad will reward everyone who's helped me, unless—"

"Unless what?" she asks

Anthony drops his eyes. "Unless he has to pay the ultimate price."

Ms. Honeycott is respectfully quiet. Then, in a voice that doesn't sound like hers at all, she asks, "You feel all right, Tony?" and he is no longer in Ms. Honeycott's office but in his own room, lying on the bed, all his clothes on, staring at the ceiling.

"You feel all right, Tony?" Mrs. Diamond asked again.

"I've got a little headache."

"You want to take something for it?"

"No. I'll be okay if I get a little rest."

"I didn't expect your dad to run off like that."

"He had no choice."

She stared at him as if she thought that a strange answer. "Did you get his address?"

He deliberately ignored the question. "I think if I don't talk for a while my headache will go away."

Rebuffed, she stood there for a moment, a worried expression on her face. Then she went over to the window and lowered the shade to darken the room. From the foot of the bed, she took the comforter, opened it and placed it over him. "You just have yourself a nice rest. If you still don't feel good at supper time, I'll bring up a tray."

"I won't want anything to eat."

"We'll see," she said, then left him to the dark quiet of the room.

He thought of Ms. Honeycott again and of what he would tell her. The truth, of course. "My dad has a couple of good job possibilities lined up. He'll be settled by fall. Then we'll get a house and a housekeeper and everything will be like old times." That's what he'd tell her. And it *was* the truth. His dad had said so. He lay there, his head in a muddle, yet feeling very tired. He closed his eyes and tried to make his mind a blank. After a long time, he fell asleep.

The next thing he knew, light flooded the room. He glanced around with foggy eyes to see Hildy, a tray in her hands. "Mom says you can eat up here," she said.

"I'm not hungry."

She ignored him. "Sit up."

Anthony sat up. He pulled a pillow from beneath the bedspread and shoved it behind his back. She gingerly set the tray on his lap. He looked down at his invalid food, scrambled eggs and toast, carrot and celery sticks, fresh fruit and milk. His mouth felt dry. "Maybe I'll just have a piece of celery."

Hildy helped herself to a carrot stick and sat on the

edge of the bed. "I've been perishing to talk to you."

"Perishing?"

"Yes—to find out what happened. Mom said I wasn't to bother you until you felt better. Is your headache gone?"

"Headache? Oh. Oh, I guess."

"Good. Then tell me all about it."

Anthony crunched on the celery. "Nothing to tell."

"Was it a secret mission?"

He scowled. "Yeah, big secret."

"You mean it wasn't? What's he been doing?"

"I can't talk about it."

Hildy chewed on the carrot and regarded him gravely. Finally she said, "You going to live with him?"

"In the fall."

"Oh." Her voice sounded solemn.

"Yeah. You see, he's got a couple of terrific job possibilities lined up. By fall, everything will break. Then we'll get a house and a housekeeper and it'll be like old times." He concentrated on his plate and became very absorbed in his scrambled eggs.

"Did you ever have a housekeeper?"

"Well, no."

"Then how can it be like old times?"

Irritated, he said, "Well, it just can, that's all."

She was quiet for a moment. Then she said, "I'll sure miss you."

"You will?"

"Well, sure. I won't have anyone to talk to. And

Mom will miss you. And Dad—I don't know what he'll do. He'll never go fly that stuff all by himself."

"It's not stuff—it's a Stuka." With his fork, he piled his eggs into one big mound.

"All during supper that's all we talked about. Did your father have a job? Was he going to take you away? And nobody knowing what to think because you wouldn't tell them. Dad's really been climbing the walls. He wanted to come right upstairs when he got home, but Mom wouldn't let him."

"Really?"

"Yes. And when he finds out you're leaving in the fall—" Hildy sighed. "I guess there'll be no living with him. He's been a lot better since he started the flying. I don't know—I guess maybe he's getting rid of his energy on something besides me."

"Did *you* notice that? I thought so, too." Without thinking Anthony scooped up a mouthful of eggs and swallowed. They went down hard. "You know, you could always get another foster."

"Maybe. But it's hard to get used to somebody new."

"That's true." And it *was* true. He'd thought he would never get used to Hildy. Yet she didn't even look squinty to him any more. And right now she looked a little sad. She really would miss him. Both Hildy and Mom. And Mr. Diamond would never fly the Stuka again, never test his skill in radio-control.

A deep rich sadness came over Anthony. He visualized himself dead, lying in a casket, the way he dimly remembered his mother. The Diamonds were leaning over, looking at his still face. Mrs. Diamond was saying, "They'll be glad to get a nice boy like Tony in heaven." Mr. Diamond was saying, "Nobody could bring in a plane for a three-point landing the way Tony could." Hildy was saying, "He really had a good sense of humor."

That was the way it had been with his mother— neighbors, friends, saying all the nice things they remembered about her. He wanted to say to Hildy now, "You'll get over it—you really will." At first you don't believe it at all. Every morning for a long time he'd kept thinking that his mother would be there in the kitchen when he came downstairs. Then one day he stopped thinking about it, stopped expecting it. The kitchen was no longer a room without his mother. It was only a room.

"When is he coming back?"

Anthony, still deep in his funereal fantasy, said, "He's never coming back. He's dead."

"Dead!" Hildy said. "You're not even listening to me. I asked you when your dad was coming back."

Anthony roused himself to stare at her for a moment. Then he said, "I don't think he's coming back."

"Ever?"

"Ever." The words had popped out of his mouth before he was aware he was even thinking them. Now that he'd said them, he was sure they were true. His dad would never come for him any more than Gran's son would ever come for her. He felt a big ache inside him, something he knew would be with him for a long time. Yet one day, he supposed, the kitchen would again be only a kitchen.

"I don't understand you," Hildy said. "You mean he's going to send someone else to get you in the fall?"

"No."

"Then how are you going to live with him?"

"I'm not."

"I *really* don't understand you—if you're not going to live with him, where *are* you going to live?"

"Here. As long as you all want me."

"Here? You mean it?"

"Uh huh."

"Then why did you say what you did?"

"Well, I—I— I really don't feel like talking about it right now. Maybe tomorrow. Okay?"

Hildy looked unsatisfied, but she offered a slightly reluctant, "Okay," then said, "Can I tell Mom and Dad you're not leaving?"

Mom and Dad would certainly want to know. And so would Ms. Honeycott. "Sure."

Hildy helped herself to another carrot stick. "You know something? I'm really thrilled that you're staying."

And Hildy really did look thrilled. That made Anthony feel a little better. And that reminded him. "I forgot to tell you. I know something else that will thrill you."

But he was wrong. When he told her about Dodger

Stadium, she wasn't thrilled at all this time. She was ecstatic.

After feeling so gloomy, Anthony couldn't help but catch a little of her mood. After all, he wasn't dead and lying in a casket. He was alive and living with people who really seemed to want him. And that was something. He said, "After school tomorrow, you want to go over and visit Sincere?"

"Sure. I adore playing with him."

"Me, too." Anthony figured he and Sincere had a lot in common. So did he and Gran. He thought of the chocolates he had once wanted to buy her. He thought of his money box. He thought about it hard for a long moment. Then he said, "You know what I want to do after we visit Sincere?"

"What?"

"Well, I've been saving some money. We'll go over to the shopping center and buy Gran a box of chocolates and another box for the family."

"Oh, she'll really be thrilled. Me, too. But do you have that much money?"

"More," Anthony said. "I keep it in my Chinese puzzle box." He moved his tray off his lap and got up. "I'll show you. I'll even show you how the box works. But you'll never remember. It's too complicated."

Anthony took the box from his drawer and, step by step, took Hildy through the complex procedure that opened it.

Hildy was really thrilled.